THE DEX-FILES

AN EXPERIMENT IN TERROR NOVELLA 5.7

KARINA HALLE

D1362023

Copyright © 2012 by Karina Halle

First edition published by Metal Blonde Books

Second edition published 2020

All rights reserved.

No part of this book may be reproduced in any form or by any electronic or mechanical means, including information storage and retrieval systems, without written permission from the author, except for the use of brief quotations in a book review.

Cover: Hang Le Designs

Edited by: Laura Helseth

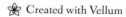 Created with Vellum

For all my pervy weirdos (yes, you!)

INTRODUCTION

Greetings my fair readers. You are about to go where very
few people have gone before – inside the mind of Declan
"Dex" Foray. I must warn you that if you haven't read all
the books in the Experiment in Terror Series (including
OLD BLOOD! It's very important to understanding this
book, all the books), put down your e-reader and go do so
now. Go on. I'll wait.

If you have read all the books, feel free to carry on. I
wouldn't want the series (which is told from Perry
Palomino's POV) to be spoiled for anyone.

Now, I must warn you that Dex's head is not always a
pretty place. You probably know that already and that's
why you love him (or want to kill him. Same difference). It's
a place that sometimes doesn't make sense. One minute it's
dark and terrible, the next it's completely smutty and
perverted. I tried to clean it up but you know what – you
can't bleach this man's brain. So, if you're OK with graphic
sex, swearing and the usual Dex Foray, fuckery, well...I
think you're in for a treat.

PROLOGUE

I was six years old when I got my first taste of hell.

I woke up to a horrible howling noise, like a dog caught in the throes of deep emotional pain, agony that went beyond the physical. It was chilling. Terrifying. Like, make your balls shrivel up into pricks of ice sort of terror. It quickly plucked away whatever ignorance my sleep had thrust on me and slapped me in my young face. This wasn't a dream. This was as real as all hell. There was a monster in my house, the kind that preyed on little boys, but it wasn't under my bed or in my closet. It was next door. Or, as it seemed to be, the floor below, scratching and howling its way from the kitchen.

It was my mother. And from the sounds of glass breaking and furniture scuffling, my dad had found her. The howling intermixed with his booming voice, his threats, his pathetic cries that betrayed the collected man he was always trying to be. It sounded ugly. It always sounded ugly but tonight I was especially scared. When a vicious cry was followed by the sound of someone being shoved into a wall,

I'm not ashamed to say I promptly wet myself. Pissing your pants seemed like the only thing to do when the monster was loose and I made a silent, naïve prayer to the man upstairs, praying that it was my mother who was thrown against the wall. I'm callous, maybe. I've been called worse. But if it were my father, and he was out cold, she'd come looking for me next.

I thought about pulling the covers over my head and hiding from it all like a coward, but that never worked. I would pretend all I could that my blanket was my invisible cloak and it would shelter me from everything bad in the world, but I learned at a very young age that there was no such thing as shelter. Maybe I would have been safer if I didn't care. Maybe indifference could have been my protector. But I still loved – and feared – my parents. That love is what scared me. It gave them the upper hand. They sure as fuck didn't love me.

I heard a shuffling from outside my door, slow and light. It was only Michael, though it rattled my wee body to think things were bad enough that *he* got out of bed. Michael was just three years older but he might have well been another decade. He was the golden boy, the child of light. I was the runt, the child of dark. I feared. Michael didn't.

I quickly jumped out of bed and scurried across to the door, purposely missing the part of the floor that I knew squeaked. I turned the knob silently and saw Michael's shadow just down the hall, heading toward the stairs. Half of him was lit up by a dying night light.

He stopped as soon as he heard me and though I could barely see it, I could *feel* the look. It said *go back to bed, you'll get us in trouble.* Only I could get us in trouble just by being awake. I still don't know why my mother had it in for me. Sometimes I think she saw a lot of herself in me, even at

2

such an age. That's a fucking terrifying thought. I'd be lying if I said that, and other things, didn't keep me up at night.

That look though from Michael, that was the most I'd ever seen him scared. It felt good, selfishly good, to know he wasn't inhuman, that he feared things too. Maybe not the way I did, but hell if I hadn't been wondering if my brother was born without a soul. Now I knew he was just older and better at hiding it than me.

I opened my mouth to say something but he placed his finger to his lips. We listened. The wailing had stopped. There was no more noise.

The fresh piss felt cold against my legs and I was suddenly, acutely embarrassed of what I had done. It's damn funny how Michael had that effect on me.

Even funnier was how I remember reaching out for his hand, looking for some sort of pathetic comfort in my blood relative, my Mikey. He jumped as if my very touch startled him or scathed his skin. Yet he let me hold his hand, even though it was tiny and clammy and I grasped him hard, until bone rubbed against bone. I never felt as grateful to my brother as I did at that moment, for not letting go. Yeah the asswipe would let go later. Fuck, he'd order up my own execution if he could (don't think he wouldn't try). But at that moment, I wasn't alone.

We made our way down the stairs, holding hands. You'd think it would be less scary without the yelling and the damn woman howls, but the silence was hazed with suspense and unheard threats. And forget the smell of urine emanating from me, I was *this* close to shitting myself.

When we reached the floor we heard a very slight tinkling of glass. We both froze and Michael's grip on mine intensified. Just for a second. But it was enough.

The sound was followed by a groan. Then a flopping

3

sound of body and skin against shiny tiled floors. This wasn't good. This was very, very bad.

I wanted to turn and run. I think I may have tried. But Michael held me there and we both watched as a dark figure came crawling out of the door to the kitchen. She moved on the floor like a drunk snake. That's what she was, after all. A fucking drunk snake out to eat us alive.

She didn't get far. Her arms were outstretched and reaching for us but she got two feet before she gave up and passed out. She smelt like wine and evil. Like sweat and sadness. Of all the feelings that hit me at that moment, I felt...bad. Looking back, I pitied her.

Michael and I stood there, staring dumbly at our unconscious mother. Michael's eyes were hard in the darkness, tiny pinpricks in the black. I wonder, did he feel hate toward her? Did he still love her? Did he feel loved? Or was he as confused as I was, forever mixing up love and hate and fear and females. I'll never know. I don't think I even care.

The spell of shock wore off when we heard another sound from the kitchen. My father was stirring. My first instinct was to run and hide. I feared him in a different way. That I'd get a spanking for wetting my pjs. That I'd be told I was nothing but a fuck up (not so much in those words, I was six after all, but I got the gist. I'm no dummy). But he didn't notice in the darkness. He appeared in the doorway, standing over my mother, with an expression of hopelessness and utter disdain on his face. *This is what I get*, it said.

Instead he said, "You boys are getting a nanny. We can't live like this."

Same difference, I suppose.

My name is Dex Foray and I'm a hypocrite. Proud of it, too. I call my mother a monster but I'm the one who took her last name. Maybe because unlike my dad, she never left me. There's something to be said for sticking around...even if it kills you.

I'm a hypocrite because I can't stand weakness in others, even though I'm born of weakness myself. I dish it out and then laugh when they try and dish it back. Like I'm above it. And sometimes I think I am.

I'm a hypocrite because I hunt ghosts and I've pretended all this time that the ghosts haven't been hunting me.

And I'm a hypocrite because I judge people. I judge the fuck out of everyone I meet, from their music tastes, to their jobs to their lifestyle choices. I judge them but fuck them if they dare judge me. They think they understand this monster in me, the monster in all of us. But they don't.

They don't know where I've come from.

They don't know my side of the story.

But now you do.

ONE

AFTER SCHOOL SPECIAL

"Hey Dex. Way to fuck my girlfriend, you dick!"

That was the only warning I had before Chase Huntington – steroid monkey and douchefucker extraordinaire – punched me right in the face. I don't know if you've ever had a fat, pharmaceutically pumped fist meet your eyebrow ring and eye socket at the same time but I gotta tell you, it's not fun.

There was a black explosion of pain and I stumbled backward and hit the wall, dropping my joint to the ground. My friend Toby gasped and I couldn't tell if the fuck was upset about the joint or that his bandmate was injured. I was seeing stars out one eye and squinting angrily at Chase with the other.

"What the hell was that for?" I cried out as Toby quickly scooped up the joint from near my feet.

"Are you fucking deaf?" Chase bellowed, taking a step forward, his fist raised.

Oh right. The whole girlfriend fucking thing.

It was true. Not a misunderstanding by a long shot. But

7

I was going to play it that way, especially as I saw the hungry eyes of our nearby classmates focus on us from across the yard, sniffing the potential blood in the air. Kids, they always liked a fight, especially one between a jock and a skid like me. This was David and Goliath level here, people. One scrawny, pierced 15-year-old fuck-up against an 18-year-old who failed high school twice because he couldn't spell his name properly.

I mean, what, they were really going to believe that Amanda Layne, Chase's gorgeous, straight-A student, gymnastics champion girlfriend would sleep with someone like me?

Well she did. Don't ask how I did it. I think I give off some kind of "I don't give a fuck" charm or maybe it's the long hair and eyebrow ring. Or maybe it's because I'm very, very persistent and I more or less cornered her in the dark-room after photography class and shoved my tongue down her throat and gave her a taste of something she couldn't say no to. A Dex sample, totally free. She didn't have to buy the thing, but she did.

I'm a good product.

For whatever reason it worked and a few days ago I was going down on Amanda underneath the bleachers (yeah, yeah how cliché but chicks dig clichés). I think I ate as much dirt as I did pussy but she seemed to like it. No, scratch that, *love* it. I could tell from the way she screamed out my name until I had to put my hand over her mouth in case someone heard us. The bleachers soon led to her car (she's a year older) and I took some perverse pleasure in the fact that I was screwing something Chase prized very dearly. It made me feel like I was *The Shit*. She wanted me. He wanted her. I walked away clean.

Or at least I had until Chase found me during lunch hour. I knew this was coming, I just had hoped I wasn't stoned at the time so I could have had a little more warning. I could have devised a better plan than the one that came into play.

"How dare you accuse me of something like that?!" I hollered back in mock disgust and rubbed at my eye which I knew was going to be black and swollen very soon. "I wouldn't touch that skank with a ten-foot pole."

Big mistake.

The gathering crowd gasped.

"Dude," Toby said under his breath before toking away.

This time I did see the fist coming. I planned on it. No guy worth their salt wants to hear their girlfriend being called a skank.

Chase lunged for me, but I was smaller and went lower. I tackled him at the waist and it was only surprise that allowed me to knock him off his feet. We hit the ground and fumbled for a bit until I managed to straddle him much like I wanted Amanda to straddle me (she was too shy or some girly bullshit) and I delivered a few quick jabs to his jaw and a crushing one to the nose. He cried out in pain at the crunch and blood and then literally threw me off of him.

I rolled for a few feet expecting to have Chase's over-puffed Nike sneakers crushing my face at any second but there was nothing. I opened my eyes and blinked at the sky. Something was blocking it. Something fat and round like the sun.

Principal Gould.

From what he saw, the scruffy, troublesome Dex Foray had randomly attacked Chase Huntington, one of the star football players and heroes of the school. No wonder Chase kept failing. Why leave a place where even the principal worshipped the ground you walked on?

I (barely) had the chance to defend myself physically but there was no way I could do so by talking. I opened my mouth to say something, anything, but Gould shot me that look that said I would only harm myself more by talking.

I took my chances.

"He attacked me!" I protested, trying to get up to my feet. I shot Chase a look and wasn't surprised to find him shrugging and looking totally innocent. I then looked to Toby.

"Tell him what happened," I said frantically.

"Uhhhh," Toby said through glazed eyes and at that moment we realized that getting in a fight wasn't our biggest problem. Toby was caught red-handed with a joint in his hands. I admired the balls (or blunted stupidity) on the kid because instead of sticking up for me he puffed on the joint at supersonic speed before Gould snatched it out of his mouth.

"You boys are coming with me."

I had been at my new high school for two years now but time hadn't eased anything. I had been happy at my old school in Manhattan, happy with my life before my pa decided to up and go. Leave me and my brother Michael behind with nothing but our crazy mother. OK, maybe not happy as a "pig in the shit" type happy but I was certainly *happier*. Here, in Brooklyn, I never found my place. I coasted through life fucking around, barely going to classes, doing a lot of drugs fifteen-year-olds should never do, doing a lot of girls fifteen-year-olds should never do. Ha.

At my new school I came in as the brooding, mysterious fuck-up and I remained that way in the eyes of everyone,

Principal Gould especially. This wasn't my first fight either. The first day of school some drooling asshole found out I had come from the Upper West Side and said I was a tight-assed prepster. How the hell he got tight-assed prepster from my uniform of cargo pants, Misfits tee shirt and boots was beyond me, but it pissed me off enough to lay the smack down on him. Unfortunately, the drooling asshole was also bigger than me and that fight ended with my face in the dirt. Still, my reputation as being a scrapper was sealed.

Gould ushered us into his office, the dungeon of doom as we liked to call it, and gave us a threatening lecture that made his cheeks puff out and turn all red. He said he was going to call our parents...actually he shot one look at me and decided that Toby was the bigger issue here.

It was a smart move. My mom would have been drunk on her ass and he would have gotten an earful from her. As much of a mess as my mother was, you didn't fuck with her children. Only *she* could fuck with her children.

So Toby's mother heard all about how her son broke the law by smoking pot at school. Of course Principal Gut had to bring me into it any way he could and made it sound like I was the bad influence on Toby. Phhfff. Toby was bad before I even showed up.

I'm not sure how much Toby's mom, who was a whippet-shaped dream muncher, really cared about the fact that I got in a fight and it must have gotten through to Gould, because when he was done with her, hanging up the phone in a sweaty huff, he looked at us both with frustration.

"You're both suspended for the rest of the week," he growled. "Go home."

Woo hoo! All right! No school!

That's what most kids would say. I mean, with suspension you had the lecture and grief and disappointment from your parents, but after that you didn't have to go to school, and your classmates would talk about you for months like you're a real bad ass.

Notice I said most kids. That wasn't the case for me.

I actually liked school. No, wait, I take it back. I actually liked *being* at school. Classes and teachers could kiss my perky ass, but school wasn't home. And any place that wasn't home was a place I wanted to be. My mother worked nights and she was home during the day. It was bad enough having to see her for a couple of hours after class where, if I was lucky, she'd throw a cheap frozen meal in the microwave for me and Michael. If I wasn't lucky, Michael would be out with his friends, my mom would be in rage mode, and I'd have a belt mark on my neck for looking at her wrong.

I exchanged a grim look with Toby, who no doubt would be grounded during his suspension and thus no band practice nor access to weed. This was going to suck.

In the months to come, I'd look back at that moment and want to pull my hair out. I wanted to yell at myself, tell myself to not go home. Go anywhere else. I wanted to hold onto that feeling that things couldn't get any worse when they very well could. I wanted that ignorance back.

But there was no turning back.

I went home. I was hungry and bored and even though I hung out at my favorite record store for a few hours, killing time, my house was calling me.

I knew it was a mistake the minute I walked in. Our place was small as all hell, with sad, peeling blue walls that looked silly against the relatively fancy furniture that we salvaged after dad left. The apartment normally had this moldy smell about it, like death clung to the walls, but that evening it was another smell. It was the stench of melted plastic and it stung my nostrils something bad.

I quietly placed my backpack on the floor and shut the front door behind me. Living in an apartment was hard when you had a mom who liked to scream and yell and cry and puke a lot. The neighbors, even the drug dealers, must have hated us. I had this weird feeling that this was going to be another epic disturbance and I hoped the other tenants weren't home.

The next thing I found weird, aside from the gross stench, was the silence. Usually the TV was blaring, or you could hear the sound of my mom pouring herself a drink, or she was yammering en Français to far-off distant relatives who didn't want anything to do with her nonsense.

But there was nothing.

It was fucking creepy.

I crept down the hallway, wishing I'd worn my Vans to school instead of the combat boots. Wherever my mom was, she knew I was coming.

I looked in the kitchen. Empty.

I peeked in her room. Empty.

I peeked in Michael's room. Empty

I stopped outside my door. It was closed. I always closed it but I knew she was in there. The god-awful smell of burning plastic filtered out from under the doorframe.

Along with a tuft of smoke.

Holy fucking shit.

I put my hand on the knob and before I could hesitate any longer, I whipped the door open.

My mother was on her hands and knees in the middle of my room. I had a terrible sense of déjà vu, like I'd seen this before. My mother wasn't very original with her drunken terrorizing.

But that's not what caused my heart to fill with ice. That's not what made my skin crawl with disgust and righteous, bubbling over anger.

All of my records were sprawled out on the floor in front of her. My precious vinyl collection that I had worked for so long to acquire, paid for with the paltry change I scrounged up over the years. The music my mother said was the work of the devil.

She hadn't said that lightly. It turns out she very much believed it for my mother was lighting my records on fire. Let me repeat that. She was lighting my fucking record collection on *fire*. Half of them were reduced to a nauseating pile of melted black vinyl, producing a stench that made my eyes water. Maybe I was crying too, I don't know. Call me a wimp for shedding a tear, but those records meant absolutely everything to me and she was destroying them.

"I'll cast you out!" she screamed with a wicked smile, holding a lighter in one hand and Pink Floyd's *The Wall* in another. She was destroying it and loving it.

I don't know how long I stood there in stupor as the smoke began to flood the room. She had left the window open but it wasn't helping. The carpet around the melted records began to flicker a little from budding flames. My room was about to turn into an inferno if I didn't do something.

It was a tough call. I wanted to save my records, what was left of them. I wanted to prevent my room from going up in flames. And I wanted to go over there and hit her so bad. And fuck you if you think that's wrong. I was so angry at her and this horrible thing she'd become. Angry that I came from her and angry that she made my dad leave and angry that she always loved Michael, but not me.

Never me.

I didn't hit her, even though it would have been karma for beating me up all these years. I gathered my wits at the last minute and ran out of the room and to the kitchen. The rage was blinding me, taking over but I had to think. THINK! I needed to get water to the fire and fast.

I pulled out a bucket from under the sink and flipped on the rusted tap. The water wasn't coming out fast enough. Fucking plumbing in the building had always sucked.

I heard her coming behind me.

Please don't come any closer, I thought to myself, closing my eyes and gripping the bucket even harder. I was afraid what would happen if she did.

I turned and looked. She was walking unsteadily toward me, her clothes stained with ash and grease. She pointed at me, fixing her dark eyes on mine. Oh how I wished I didn't look so much like her.

"Mom, go away!" I cried out, my voice cracking shamefully. I looked back to the bucket. Half-full. Just a few more seconds.

"You're not my son," she said in this low, utterly deranged voice. "You're not my son."

Fuck, this again? If I had a nickel for every time she told me I wasn't her son, I'd be able to re-buy my record collection.

I caught a whoosh of sound from around the corner and beyond my mother's sad form, there was a hint of light on the walls. The fire was growing. The bucket would have to do for now.

I lifted it out of the sink, the water spilling to the sides.

"I wasn't me when I had you."

That one was new.

I turned around and looked at her, the water sloshing in my hands and dripping to my feet.

"Mom, please I have to put out the fire."

I took a few steps forward hoping to walk past her. But she came toward me, putting her body in between myself and the fire. I tried not to look at her eyes, tried not to see the madness and shame in them, but I was doing exactly that.

"I wasn't me when I had you. I wasn't me! You're not my son!" she bellowed, her rotten, booze-filled breath blowing hotly in my face.

"Get out of my way mom, please," I begged, my voice wavering. We didn't have time for her lunatic rantings. She wasn't herself? What did that even mean?

"I wasn't me when I had you!" she screamed.

"Mom, move!" I screamed back. I took the bucket of water and shoved it against her.

Hard.

A little too hard.

And that was all it took. I was so angry, so out of my mind, that I shoved my mother a little too hard.

Water spilled on to the floor.

She lost her balance.

The ground was slick.

She fell backward.

She reached for me in slow motion.

I didn't drop the bucket.

I stepped back. Away from my mom's reaching hand.

She fell to the floor, almost hitting it at once.

But she had stumbled a little too close to the edge of the counter.

Her head hit the corner of it first. The sound of something being split, like a cracked watermelon, filled my ears.

Blood clung to the counter's sharp edge.

My mother landed on the floor with a thunk.

There was more blood mixing with the water, creating a pale red soup.

Then there were more flames.

Then there was nothing.

TWO

DEAR ABBY

LIFE CAN BE PRETTY SCREWY. HECTIC. RANDOM. THAT was my life anyway, and most of the time. But, occasionally, things just fall into place. There's a feeling of fate. Kismet. Order. I prefer the up-and-down jumble and unpredictability. I liked that shit happens for no reason sometimes. There's something easy about that.

When things align themselves in my favor, it makes me suspicious. Maybe because I don't like the idea of my life being part of some overall cosmic plan. I don't want the universe to pay attention to me. I just wanted to put my head down and go.

Sing Sin Sinatra (why the hell did I name it this?) had been doing really well until Toby up and left the band. Toby, my last remaining friend, a leftover from high school, decided smoking crack in the Bronx was better than playing bass in my band. OK, our band. But really, it was my band.

Not that I wouldn't have had to fire him at the rate he was going but still. It would have been my choice and my decision. Instead, just before the fall season, when we had a shit ton of shows (good shows too) to do, he decided to say see ya.

Good riddance and fuck off, said everyone else in the band. They were sick of him being late, being incoherent. He could barely play the bass anymore and that was saying a lot, especially with most of our songs. I mean, fuck, we did the classics. They were as simple as shit. But it burned me a little bit. Like I said, he was my last high school friend, a connection to my past. Did I like my past? No. I didn't even speak to my own brother anymore. But it was something.

It also sucked balls because he was going to be my editing partner. He wasn't in school, but he had the talent and the equipment. Well, before he sold it for crack. We worked well together. Well, before he started wigging out.

Fuck. I should have seen it coming.

So there I was, gathering my books, getting ready to leave my afternoon editing class. Everyone in my class was a dick so there was no way I'd feel comfortable making side projects with these people. Anyway, I needed someone who would want to fuck around with film with me. I know I'm not easy to work with, so there was that too.

I started toward the door, the last person to leave the room.

Before I got there, a gigantic red-head appeared in the doorway, panting and out of breath. A layer of sweat lay across his freckled forehead.

"I missed it didn't I?" the ginger said, his arm propping his body up against the frame. His voice was unusually smooth and he had a weird accent that was Southern but also not quite.

"Missed the class?" I asked. I walked toward him but he was still leaning against the door and his whole massive body blocked it. There was something weird about him, about the way he was, but I couldn't quite put my finger on it. Oh well, no matter. It wasn't my problem.

"Yeah. Shoot. I signed up for editing. Missed last week's too."

I gave him a false nod of sympathy. I had places to go, a girl to fuck. I wasn't about to stand around and shoot the breeze with this guy. Looking at him gave me a headache and made me want to rub my eyes vigorously. Maybe with salt.

"Better luck next week," I told him with a placating smile, then gestured for him to move.

He did. Reluctantly. I quickly glanced at him as I passed. If I'd known better, he looked confused. Maybe even hurt.

"You're Declan Foray," he called out after me.

I stopped walking. I slowly turned around.

"Yeah. Who are you?"

"Jacob." He smiled. He had pretty white teeth for a Southern boy. Then he frowned, catching himself. "No. Jacobs."

"Jacobs? With an S? Do you know your own name?" I frowned at him.

He wiped his hand on his jeans and thrust it out at me. "Maximus Jacobs."

"Oh, you have many names."

He eyed me and his hand expectantly. I sighed and dragged my ass over to him.

"Nice to meet you Maximus Jacobs. I'm *Dex* Foray." He shook my hand in a very strong, cold hold. He kept it there a little too long. I narrowed my eyes at him. He smiled in response and dropped it.

I took back my hand and wiggled it a bit. Fucker could have broken it. Who let this animal out of the zoo?

He smiled again like he'd heard what I thought and found it funny. I ignored it.

"So, Maximus Jacobs."

"Just Max, please."

"OK, Max please. How did you know who I was?"

"Word on the street was you were looking for a new bassist," he said.

"Word on the street? Who says that?" I scoffed, taking in his purple plaid shirt. "Where are you from?"

"The South," he said. He scratched at his orange sideburns. He had a very wannabe Elvis type do. It looked stupid.

"Oh, the South," I remarked dryly. "Always wanted to go there."

A smile tugged at the corner of his mouth. "Louisiana. Outside of New Orleans. On the coast."

OK. Now his accent went from odd and slightly Southern to full-on Cajun. Like he was trying to sound neutral but eventually failed.

I needed a cigarette badly. I sighed and pinched the bridge of my nose. I don't know where the headache had come from but it was apparent that standing around talking to the burly Cajun wasn't helping. Still, I had to know.

"So you say word on the street?" I mused. "Who told you?"

He shrugged. "I just overheard."

So, so vague. "All right. Do you play bass?"

He smiled broadly. He almost looked angelic. "I play everything but I love bass."

Did anyone really love the bass? I mean, I could play everything too. I loved the sound of the bass but playing the bass? Unless you were peeling off some Les Claypool riffs, it was boring as fuck.

"I can play just like Les Claypool."

I flinched. "What?" Had I said that shit out loud?

"Les Claypool. You know, he's in Primus."

"Yes, I know who he is," I snapped. I eyed him warily. "You don't know what kind of music we play. It's not exactly Primus."

He nodded. "I know. I've seen you live."

That startled me. Did I have a stalker here?

"When?" I demanded.

He shrugged. "When I first got here."

"Our last show was a month ago..."

"Then I got here a month ago. Look, I really liked your band."

I could see how sincere he was. But still.

Reading the doubt on my face, he quickly said, "I'll even audition. I reckon I'll win you over yet."

He'll *reckon*? My god, why didn't he just stick to the banjo and pots and pans? Fucking hillbilly. Still, we needed a bassist and finding one in New York City that wasn't either an asshole professional or drooling crackhead wasn't easy. My bandmates might even like the jolly red giant.

"Thank you," he said.

"I didn't say anything," I muttered, annoyed and feeling deflated.

"I know. I could just tell. Do you smoke?" he asked.

I perked up. "Fuck yes."

He fished a packet of cigarettes out of his shirt pocket. They were in a bright yellow box, with Spanish writing. "Ever had Cuban cigarettes?"

"No. How did you get those?"

"I have ways. Come on," he nodded toward the exit and I was suddenly aware that there was a school around me with students and teachers going back and forth. It was the

22

weirdest fucking thing, like I'd been in a dream or something.

I had a few smokes with the Cajun. The smokes then turned into beers. Beers soon turned into jamming. I didn't need to audition him. We had our bass player. Could he play like Claypool? Not quite. But he was polite (annoyingly so), kept good time and was open to anything.

Then we got to talking about film. He had some skills in the editing department and wanted to collaborate on student films with someone. It was like god plucked Max out of the sky and handed him to me. An answer to the prayers I never made.

So, you can see why it made me suspicious. The big dude in the sky usually never gave me anything but shit. But here was Max. Ginger Elvis. A bassist and editor all in one. The perfect replacement for Toby.

Well, almost. Toby knew my history. He knew I was on some medication. He knew what made me tick. Max didn't know any of that and I fascinated him for some reason. He was always asking me questions. Questions I didn't want to answer, like about my parents. About my brother. What my childhood was like. Did I have any nannies growing up. Who were my friends.

Did anything strange happen to me when I was young.

"Like what?" I asked. We were sitting in a dark bar in the Bowery on a Thursday night. The weekend before we played one of our best shows yet. Seemed there were parts of New York that got the joke, the campy fun of lounge music turned rock and roll. Max and I were taking over the city.

"Oh I don't know," he said. He was eyeing a girl in the corner of the bar. She was blonde, short but pretty enough and staring at us like she knew us. I leaned my head back, looked past his shoulder at her and winked. She giggled. I knew it. She was staring at me. She was staring at me like she wanted to bend over and let me stick it anywhere.

I turned my attention back to Max. She'd be there later, and then hopefully in my bed. What Max had asked me was weird and distracting.

"Are you trying to get all serious with me?" I asked, leaning into him. "No one touched me in private places, if that's what you're getting at."

He took a sip of his drink and smiled. It was lopsided which meant he was getting drunk. It took a lot for the big guy. Almost as much as it took me.

"No, no. Just wondering if perhaps you ever experienced something supernatural," he said lightly, like it was an everyday topic.

I didn't like it. It hit way too fucking close to home. Never in a million years would I reveal the ghosts I used to see, particularly the one who tormented me the most. She had only appeared to me the night before, sticking her accusatory finger in front of my face and screaming at me until I had to fuck my way out of it. Yeah, that's right. I'm not proud of it but I'd been having a different girl in my bed for the last who knows how long. It's easy for me, to just pick them up. Chicks dig men who can sing. Fucking them is a lot of fun too but what was most important is that it distracted. It made the ghosts go away. Not always, but often. And if it didn't, well, no harm done. The girl got what she wanted, even if I didn't. At least I got laid.

I turned my attention back to the girl in the booth, suddenly afraid she'd lose interest and leave. Conjuring up the image of the ghost in my head made my blood and breath flow cold. I didn't want to be alone tonight.

I noticed Max was staring at me intently, like he was

trying to pluck my thoughts from my brain. Sometimes I thought he was the paranormal one. If not paranormal, at least a big fucking weirdo.

"What?" I asked him.

"You never replied."

"It's a dumb question." I motioned the bartender for another Jack and Coke.

"It's perfectly reasonable. Some people believe in UFOs. Others believe in ghosts. What do you believe in?"

He was still watching me, his eyes hard and patient.

I plucked my new drink off the table and took a bigger gulp than I intended. "I believe in Dex Foray. What do you believe in?"

"Dex Foray," he agreed with a smile and raised his glass. We clinked, drank the rest and that was the end of that.

Oh, and I did take the blonde home. The ghosts never came *and* I stuck my cock up her ass. Win win.

ALL RIGHT, I KNOW WHAT YOU'RE THINKING. I'M A crude man-whore. And I couldn't argue with you. If it looks like a pig and fucks like a pig, it's a pig.

But crude man-whores don't last forever. Eventually they meet someone who puts all the other women to shame. Sometimes it's someone you least expect.

Abby wasn't quite a groupie, but she certainly was a fan. I'd seen her around at shows before. She never approached me and barely looked my way half the time, but when the lights hit the room just right, I'd catch her watching me. And yes, I know, I'm the singer and everyone more or less watches me. But this was different. It wasn't lust or frenzy or acceptance I saw in her eyes. It was something akin to awe. Like she admired me. I liked that. Shit, I liked that a lot.

After one show of ours, in a tiny little club packed with more douchebags than I could count who clearly thought our band was a little more hardcore and less weird, I saw her ordering a drink by the bar. I was intrigued by this shy girl and for once I wasn't thinking with my dick.

I approached her and told the bartender that I would pay for whatever she was having.

She barely turned to face me. She just shot me a look – one I couldn't read– then turned away.

"Hey," I said. I wanted to follow it with: *I bought you a drink, say thank you.* But I didn't want to seem like an ass. So I left it at "hey" and bit my lip.

She ignored me. Walked off.

What the fuckity fuck?

I'd never had anyone do that to me. Who the hell did she think she was? She wasn't even all that pretty. She was attractive, I guess, but there was nothing remarkable about her. She had dark eyes and strawberry blonde hair that was neatly curled in waves. She was wearing a dress that was far too girly for a club and flat shoes. From what I could tell from her body, she was of average weight, not fat nor skinny, and of average height. She was pretty...average.

So why was she walking away from me? And why did I care?

Regardless, I found myself at her side again and grabbed her arm.

She looked scared. Up close, with her facing me, I could see she was a little prettier than I had originally thought. Nice lips. Nose had a bump on it. Brows were a bit too low and thick. But sparkling eyes. They made me feel kind of crazy.

"Hey," I said and smiled most handsomely. "I'm Dex."

She continued looking scared until I dropped my hand off of her arm. Then she relaxed. She took a sip of her drink.

I raised my brow and leaned into her. She smelt like soap and lavender. "Do you have a name?"

She swallowed hard and nodded. "It's Abby."

Her accent was pure Fargo. Later I'd find out it was Minnesota, but same difference.

I held out my hand. "Nice to meet you, Abby."

She gave it a light shake. It was weak but her touch lingered. I don't know what it was but I felt her touch all the way down to my toes. Now my dick twitched a bit in my pants. So much for not thinking with it.

"I hope you enjoyed the show," I said, trying to ignore the rising erection. I swear it popped up at the most inappropriate times.

"I did," she said. "I've seen all your shows."

"You're a fan?" I asked even though I knew.

"Of the band," she clarified.

"Not of me?" I teased.

She shook her head. "You're a bit of a chump."

Whoa. And my pants deflated.

I laughed awkwardly. "Ouch. Now I feel like an idiot for buying you a drink."

"I could have warned you." She smiled coyly. Was she flirting with me or wasn't she?

I eyed the drink. It was fancy looking. "I bet it was pricey too."

"Aviation club cocktail. With top shelf gin."

"Well that serves me right for assuming..."

She raised a brow. It looked less bushy now. It suited her face. She was actually very pretty. "When you assume..."

27

"You make an ass out of you and me," I supplied.

"No, I was going to say when you assume, you make assumptions."

I grinned at her. "Aren't you a clever girl?"

She looked down at the floor and in the dim light I caught a hint of color growing on her face. Success! I made her blush. "I've been called worse things."

I held out my arm for her. "Well since you're such a fan of the band, would you like to meet them?"

She nodded excitedly. "Yes please. Especially Max."

I kept the smile on my face while I frowned internally. Wasn't easy. Fucking Max. This wasn't the first time girls were going after him. It pained me to admit it but he was one good looking dude. But it was the first time a girl I wanted showed interest in him.

A girl I wanted. There you had it. And it wasn't just in a fuck your brains out till morning, avoid the ghosts and get the goods, type of want, either. Oh it was there, but I had a strange inkling to actually spend some time with this girl. Talk to her. Figure out what she's about. *Then* fuck her brains out.

But I sucked it up. I brought Abby over to meet Max, even though he was dating a girl named Kate at the time. I also introduced her to Dennis (our drummer), Travis (our guitarist) and Pete (our keyboardist). She was actually quite shy and reserved around all of them but they were nice enough and Pete even bought her another one of her weird gin cocktails.

She flirted with Max all night, sitting on his lap and giggling into his ear as she got progressively drunker. Something told me that she was drinking to cover up what she was feeling. Shyness? Nervousness? Either way, even though she wasn't in my care or even my friend, I felt strangely protective of her.

At one point we were in the back room of the club with our gear and Abby and Max had started making out. He was drunk too, so I had to go over and tap him on the shoulder and very clearly say, "Where's Kate? You know, your girlfriend?"

That barely got his attention. So I tapped Abby on the shoulder. "You should probably go home Abby. Come on I'll call you a cab."

She pushed me away but eventually Max came to his senses and put an end to it. I didn't want him to take her anywhere because that wouldn't have ended well, so I put my arm around her and escorted her to road.

She stumbled a bit, drunk as anything. A cab came up but I realized I didn't have the heart to send her on her way. I didn't know where she lived and she probably wouldn't know either. She was that wasted.

With a sigh I got in the cab with her and we left for my apartment. That was the beauty about being the singer. Never had to help the band load in and out. I just showed up and left as I pleased.

Believe it or not, we didn't have sex. I wasn't an animal. She ended up with her head in the toilet most of the night just puking her guts up. And yes, I held her hair back. She was right. I was a total chump.

But whatthefuckever. I guess it bonded us or something because after that we were inseparable. We had sex the following morning and didn't stop for days, weeks, months. I only stopped to eat, shit, go to school, drink, play a show, write a song, make a movie. Every other spare moment we were in each other's beds, screwing like our livelihoods depended on it, as if we were trying save humanity with each moan, with each thrust.

It was a good few months. The best.

Then things started to change. I started to change. Abby had gotten under my skin. She was all I thought about, all I wanted to do. I was addicted to her, physically and mentally. I was obsessed. I was paranoid. I was jealous. I was head over heels in love. So far down the rabbit hole that there no way out. I was wedged in there, helpless and needy. Oh so fucking needy.

It...disgusted me.

No one had done that to me before. I had never given a girl that type of power. I didn't trust females. I didn't want them close to me. I wanted them close enough that I could see their eyes flutter when they came but I didn't want them inside me. I was inside them - it wasn't the other way around. I didn't want them anywhere near my soul or my heart but fucking Abby, she clawed her way in and set up camp.

The Dex Foray I knew was gone. If I thought I was out-of-control before, I was wrong. I was always in control. Wild but on purpose. Crazy but free. With Abby I was locked down and trapped because I couldn't go a single day without feeling her wetness around me, without looking into her deep eyes, begging her for some sort of acceptance.

I'd fallen. And it sucked.

And really, it was my fault. I gave into love and it chewed me up and spit me out.

I became a man I never wanted to be and I drove her away.

I accused her of cheating on me when she wasn't. And when she inevitably did, I blamed it on myself. So did she. Or, I guess she did. I never knew because she died.

Another death on my hands.

I forget all the details. It doesn't matter that she drove drunk and had many DUIs before back in Minnesota. It didn't matter that I was just the angry boyfriend and she had been having an affair. It didn't matter. She's dead. My fault through and through.

I'd never experienced such pain in my entire life. And that was saying a lot. Losing Abby...I lost a part of my own life. My own future. There was chunk of my heart and soul buried with her in that cold, cold ground and I was never, ever going to get that back.

And Max. Where was he in all this? He was my closest friend, the guy who was always around, like a flame-haired shadow, asking me questions about weird things, taking me out for a drink when Abby and I had a fight (which, by the way, was often). He went from, I don't know, a (shitty) guardian angel, or even a brother figure, to someone who despised me. Maybe that's not the word. He was disappointed in me. It's like he gave up and decided I wasn't the type of person he wanted to be around anymore. I thought Max being in my life was fate. An answer to something.

I couldn't have been more wrong.

To make matters worse, because he was pushing me away, I found comfort in his girlfriend, Kate. At first she was just a shoulder to cry on. She was Abby's best friend now too and she was also hurting. Eventually though, things got physical. Max thinks I only slept with her once, and that's because he caught us in a very compromising position. The truth is, I was sleeping with Kate every chance I could.

Because, you see, the ghosts were back. I didn't have Abby to distract me from them.

This time, the ghost *was* Abby.

THREE

SPOOKSHOW BABY

THE ROOM SMELLED LIKE SHIT. SHIT, SEAWEED AND decades of decay. It was too bad Smell-O-Vision never went anywhere, because the smell of the old lighthouse would have been just as terrifying as the sight of it.

Speaking of, there wasn't much to see here. Downstairs was empty. This floor gave up nothing except doors that wouldn't open and I was beginning to doubt Old Captain Fishsticks was actually haunting the place. Just because pansy-assed ghost hunting shows were clamoring to film the lighthouse, didn't mean anything was actually here. Had I been duped by the hype? No. Not me. That was impossible.

I stopped in the middle of the room and sighed, the camera feeling extra heavy on my shoulder. A migraine tickled my temples and I pinched the bridge of my nose, hard. I hated feeling like a fuck-up failure. I couldn't go back to Jimmy empty-handed. I suppose I could, seeing as the asshole didn't really know what I was up to, but it didn't matter. He'd sniff it off of me like some fucking dog. He'd know I was down here, trying to find something better for myself.

Then there was Jenn. She was worse. She said she was sad when I left the show, but I could see through those tears of hers. I knew what they meant. She was secretly pleased I took off with the tail between my legs, like she won yet another battle or something. Three years with someone and you get to know their tactics pretty well. You can see that smug smile beneath the "But I'll miss you." The one that says I'll be nothing without her, that I'll fail on my own.

I didn't want Jenn to be right. But looking around this disgusting, dark relic with the kelp and the crashing waves outside, waves that seemed to laugh at me, well, fuck, she probably was right. Again.

I chewed on my lip absently and looked above. I had more of this place to see. I wasn't going to give up yet. After all, I was here. And even though the monsters were hidden behind veils of prescription, I was still the same boy as I was back in New York. They still wanted me, even if I couldn't see them.

My pride would be the death of me one day.

THUD.

A loud clatter sounded out from the floor below. It sounded hard, like something had toppled over from a great height.

I froze, feeling just a little spooked. I walked across the room and paused near the staircase, waiting for more.

From downstairs came a scurrying noise, like a very large rat was poking around. I carefully turned off the camera light and waited. My ears listened hard, trying to figure out just what the hell it was. From what I remembered, ghosts didn't usually make much noise. They didn't move around like they were trying to be quiet and failing at it. Rats didn't move like that either, especially not on the West Coast.

I picked up another sound now. Footsteps. Then a metallic jangling.

It was definitely a person.

I was definitely fucked.

I took in a deep breath and ignored all the possible scenarios that waited for me below. What was the point in figuring out who it was, or what was going to happen? If I got out of there without them seeing me, then worrying was fruitless.

I made my way down the stairs, pausing every other step to keep track, until I reached the bottom floor. I could hear tiny gasps of ragged breath coupled with a whimpering sound. I could see only darkness, except for weak light that spilled in through one of the rooms. There was a window where there hadn't been a window before.

You need move your ass now, I thought to myself. But before I could do anything, I felt this...this...I don't know what the hell it was, like a magnetic pull, like the air before a thunderstorm. An energy rolled toward me like a freight train. It made me stop, stunned and still.

There was another whimper, almost like a sigh, then feet slapping the damp ground.

Before I had chance to process that the footsteps were coming toward me, something collided straight into my chest. There was a scream, a girlish shriek (not my own), and I was shoved backward by something small and solid. The ground smashed into my shoulder, then my head, but it didn't matter. The CRASH of my camera was the most painful thing of all.

I groaned and rolled over, feeling for the machine.

Oh please, please, please, please, please, I thought in a panic. *I can't afford this, I can't afford this!*

I heard the other person, the beast that hit me, stirring

and moaning, then they hit the ground again with a thump that sounded painful. Part of me didn't give two shits about the asshole that might have ruined the most important thing in my life. The other part of me felt kind of bad, especially when it became apparent that the asshole was some fucking chick. She was making little terrified squeaks.

Then she made no noise at all.

Motherfucker. Now I had a broken camera and some trespassing broad who was either dead or unconscious.

I hoped she wasn't a cop.

My hand made contact with the camera, and from the initial feel I was copping, it didn't seem like much damage was done to the outside. My fingers instinctively found the light and switched it on. I let out a breath of relief as the darkness was violently illuminated.

As was the girl, lying on the ground beside me. Her eyes were closed and she wasn't moving.

Shit, shit, shit.

I got on my knees and placed my hand on her neck, feeling for a pulse. She stirred a little and moaned, which meant she was at least partially alive. Not dead. I hadn't killed her. So I had that going for me.

I couldn't see her properly in the competing darkness and blinding glare, but she seemed damn young. She was small, with a round face that glowed ghostly pale. A camera hung from her neck and onto the floor. Without thinking, I reached up and brushed a strand of black hair off of her forehead. She was warm, almost feverish. Still not dead.

At my touched she moved a little and tried to open her eyes, raising her arm up to block out the light.

"Don't move," I said, my voice coming out broken and hoarse. The last thing I needed was for her to wreck herself even further. Just because she was alive, didn't mean she was well.

She dropped her hand reluctantly and I took the light away from her face, placing the camera down on the ground beside her head. It created crazy shadows along the planes of her face. Her pert nose turned into a beak. If I let my imagination run away with me, there were a million things she could have morphed into. I was lucky I hadn't skipped my pills earlier, like I had been thinking about doing.

I touched her face again, just to make sure she was still a person. She was. She was still soft, and warm, and alive.

Was I being creepy?

Her eyes fluttered open and I could barely make out a shade of blue in them before panic tore them wider and she tried to jerk away.

I pressed her shoulder down to the ground to keep her still.

"Seriously," I told her. "You might be really hurt. Please don't move."

She obeyed and lay back down.

"I'm OK," she said through dry lips. Her voice was light and scared. But she didn't sound like she was in any trauma. Her eyes searched my face without really seeing me.

I still had one hand on her shoulder and the other on her face.

I was definitely being creepy.

I took my hands away and inched back a bit to give her space to breathe - and me space to run. She looked no older than 20, so she obviously wasn't a cop but she was here, in a place I had no right to be. I eyed the hall in the darkness, wondering if getting out of the building was going to be as hard as getting in. I hoped she wasn't about to call for help. Or press charges.

She eased herself up and looked warily around the darkness, her eyes focusing on the camera. I could see the wheels turning behind those shadowed eyes, wondering what the fuck was going on.

"I'm so sorry," I said. Even though she technically ran into me, I had to placate things before they escalated.

"I was upstairs and I heard this crazy clatter from down here," I explained, my voice speeding up as my heart raced. There was too much adrenaline in my system and the medication was screwing around with it. "And I thought maybe it was the cops or something. I didn't know what the fuck to do. I thought I could get out of the way I came in, but I saw you there, and then I saw the window probably at the same time you saw the window and I'm...I'm so sorry if...well, you're obviously OK."

There was a pause. She didn't seem to buy any of that.

"Who are you?"

The million-dollar question. What would my answer be today?

"That depends on who you are," I said honestly.

In the shadows I saw her cock her brow.

"I asked you first."

Why did I have to run into the most questioning people? I exhaled and reached back into my pocket. My new business cards were printed just last week – she'd be the first person to have one.

Whoever she was.

She took it from my hands, hesitant, like I was handing her poison. So suspicious. Tsk, tsk.

I picked up the camera and aimed it at the card. It gleamed under the light. So did the chipped polish on her gothy-looking fingernails.

She read it out loud and flipped it over, then looked up

at me, somehow even more confused. The light lit up her face better.

"Are you from West Coast Living or something?"

I let out a small laugh. "Fuck no."

I started to rock back on forth on my feet, needing an outlet for the energy that was rumbling inside my bones. She was a curious little thing, but something about her made me nervous. Wary. Like she could be even more dubious than I was. Like she had a million secrets to tell and I would never hear any of them.

Whoever she was.

"Well, Dex Foray, I have a feeling that whatever you guys are doing here tonight, you're doing so without the permission of my uncle, who owns the lighthouse."

Shit. Fuck. Shit.

Her uncle owned the lighthouse. I felt the routes in my brain rewire as they prepared for the extra adrenaline, the gallop of my heart.

But...wait...

"There's no one else here," I said. "It's just me."

She laughed, clearly not believing me.

"Look, I don't care," she said and there was just enough ease in her voice to make it true. "I'm not going to report you. I shouldn't even be here myself. Just get your crew together or whatever and get out of here before you do get in trouble."

I stopped rocking. What the hell was she going on about? My crew?

"It's just me," I told her again. "Did you see someone else here?"

She frowned but kept her gaze on mine. "Yes. I heard you upstairs, and I was going to go out the window, but I saw the shadow of someone pass by. Outside."

A shudder ran down my spine and roll of nausea waved through me. I skid a bit closer to her, my pants dragging on the damp ground.

"Are you sure you saw something?"

If she had seen something, and it obviously was not me, then I was hooped up the ass. Maybe she was too, but I just couldn't get a proper reading on her. That weird energy slinked off of her in bursts and messed with my head a little bit.

"Yes, I saw someone," she said with a tinge of doubt. "Someone walked past the window, swear to god."

I wasn't sure if her god was one I could hold truth to.

"Where did you come from? Did anyone come with you?"

Like your uncle...or the cops...or your 250-pound MMA boyfriend.

She shook her head. I placed the light closer to her face, feeling like I needed to do a bit of interrogating to get to the bottom of this. She winced at the glare.

"Sorry," I mumbled. "I...well, nevermind."

"Nevermind?" she spat out. Her eyes narrowed and not from the light. "You just broke into my uncle's lighthouse. Don't you tell me to nevermind."

Whoa. All I was going to do was apologize again for doing exactly that. Well, fuck. Forget it. I was done. I was out of here.

With a grunt, I got to my feet and stretched up into the moonlight that was now creeping from the nearby window. It would be an easy escape. I picked up my foot to go, but I stopped.

I couldn't leave like this.

She looked so helpless at my feet. And I did have manners somewhere.

I reached for her hand. She eventually took it, feeling all too tiny in mine, and I brought her to her feet. She staggered a bit, almost keeling over, her camera swinging, and all I could think about was maybe she fell a lot harder than I thought. Maybe she wasn't really "all there" and we'd need an ambulance after all.

I put my hands on the sides of her arms and stepped closer to her, trying to keep her from faltering. She was short as hell and that was saying a lot since I wasn't very tall to begin with.

"You OK?" I asked, already knowing she was the type who'd say she was fine even if her limbs were chopped off. I saw a flash of something – hope? – in her eyes before she twisted us around and I was illuminated and her face was hidden in the dark. I searched out her features but couldn't get them. It was unnerving to not see the round pale face and watchful eyes.

"Just a bit dizzy," she said. The fact that she admitted that much didn't sound very good. I began to think where the nearest hospital was, whether I could get her there in the Highlander, if I would need to call her uncle first. Who would then slap me with some trespassing charges and a possible assault charge, because men were dicks and no one would believe a girl could run into me, especially not one pixie-sized.

"Good," I said, trying to look into her eyes, trying to keep things light. I smiled, thinking it might help my cause. "Promise not to sue?"

"I won't. Can't speak for my uncle, though."

Damn it! Just where was he anyway? Why was she exploring a lighthouse in the dark without him?

"Why are you here?" I asked, more and more curious about this little goth girl.

She dropped her gaze to the ground, even though I couldn't see her anyway.

"We're having a bonfire at the beach," she said. Her voice went higher, younger, and I got the distinct impression that she was feeling guilty about something. "I got sick of hanging around teenagers and wanted to come here. My uncle never let me come here when I was younger. I didn't tell anyone, I just left. I was hoping to film stuff."

Hoping to film some stuff? As if she couldn't get any more intriguing. What kind of stuff, exactly. What had she heard about the lighthouse?

She let out a small gasp and started fiddling with something. Her camera. I picked up mine and shone the light on her and while she was squinting uncomfortably at the glare, I took her SLR in my hand and peered it over. Aside from scratches that were probably there before, there was no damage.

"It's fine," I told her, trying to sound reassuring. "I thought you wrecked the shit out of mine when you ran into me."

I patted my camera which made the light bob against her face. She didn't look very impressed. Who could blame her?

"You're right," I said, before she could. "Who cares? I probably deserve to have this camera smashed."

Even though it would put me back at square one. I couldn't think about that.

Thump.

I froze. The sound had come from upstairs. Where I had just been. Where nothing else had been. Unless...

I looked at her, putting the light closer to her face. It was Bad Cop time again.

"You sure you came alone?" I whispered.

She replied, "Are you?"

I nodded. She didn't. It then occurred to me that I had no clue what her damn name was. She never offered it up. I didn't know anything about her.

This could have all been a trap. They might have known I was coming here. I don't know how, but maybe they saw the Highlander from a distance. Maybe trespassers were a weekly occurrence. Maybe they lured ghost hunters here and then robbed them. Or raped them. I'd probably let Little Miss Doe Eyes do the honors, but I had no idea how strong her uncle was.

She dropped her eyes from mine and looked at the window. The only easy way of escape.

But if she was thinking of running, that meant she was afraid. It meant she didn't know who, or what, was upstairs.

And if they didn't come with her...they were already here.

I leaned into her and smelled something like a fresh breeze radiating from her neck. It took me a moment to find my tongue, find the words to say, "Are you one hundred percent sure that no one else came with you here?"

I wanted to pull away for her response but that energy, that smell, kept my nose and mouth locked near her neck for just a few more seconds.

FOUR
EVEN DEEPER

"OH COME ON, JUST SHOOT THE FREAKING ZOMBIE already!" Matt or Tony yelled at me. I couldn't tell which one. They both looked the same and sounded the same – deafening.

I'd been playing video games with Perry's cousins for the last hour while she checked her emails and we waited for night to fall. My zombie-hunting "skills" seemed just as useless as my ghost hunting skills and the noises and the graphics were fucking up my equilibrium. I mean, shit. After what went down in the car, running into that psycho, Dame Edna lady again, I was surprised it took me this long to realize everything was doing my head in. I had enough.

"That's it," I said, throwing my controller down on the couch and getting up. "I've died for the last time."

The twins made a noise in unison. It sounded like false disappointment. It was eerie.

Then they continued playing like I had never even been there. Also eerie.

And nerdy.

I made my way over the kitchen and started to pull out

my notebook from my overnight bag. It still smelled like apple pie here, the one that Perry managed to bake earlier. What possessed her to try baking was beyond my cloudy brain. Just one more thing to scribble down on my mental notepad headlined PERRY and sort things I needed to get to the bottom of.

It was good too. Not the best thing I've tasted in my life, but it was good considering she randomly cooked it in her uncle's place. I couldn't even remember the last time I had homemade apple pie. Had I ever? The only time I could think of was the god awful Christmases with Jenn and her white-ass rich folks, and if I knew them, they probably ordered those pies from some epicurean pie catalogue for old farts.

But the thing is, it wasn't so much what it tasted like but what it smelled like. The damn pie smelled like home to me. But apple pie didn't exist in my fucked-up youth, and if it had, it wasn't at the hands of my mother. Perhaps a nanny had baked every now and then. I don't know, I didn't care to remember that shit. That whole period was blocked out for very good reasons.

But the smell still stirred up memories that never could have existed. It felt...like, warm. Good. Honest. How the hell did those things belong in my life?

I looked at Perry as she came into the kitchen and sat down at the table across from me. Her face was anxious, like she was having another battle inside that head of hers. There was something about her that stirred up the same feelings. Maybe this had nothing to do with apple pie at all. Maybe it's that she made it, and when she handed over that first slice and met my eyes, I could see she made it for me. And no one had ever made me anything.

Naturally, I wasn't about to tell her that. It was idiotic,

actually, to even think this funny little girl thought of me more than some crazy mustached fucker in her uncle's kitchen. She just met me. She didn't know me. And if she thought she did, she was mistaking me for someone else. Someone who didn't hide medication in a hollowed-out book.

I kept my mouth shut and began to write an overview of the day. I still managed to watch her at the same time, watch her debating whether to tell me something or not. A glint of something gleamed in her blue eyes. It was almost...hot. Was she thinking something naughty? I found myself shifting uncomfortably in the chair.

"So," she said, her voice high and self-conscious. "A local ghost hunter's club in Salem was hoping I could come aboard their team and perhaps show them around the lighthouse."

The...fuck? I stopped writing, trying to process what she was saying. Competition? Already? I knew I should have fucking got her to sign a contract. I knew I was being a fucksicle by just trusting that she'd stick with me and not go to someone else with this fucking access, someone who actually knew what they were doing. All that shit we said to each other in the car, all the things I said – that didn't mean shit, did it? Fuck I was a fool.

I cleared my throat and tried to sound casual. "And?"

She shrugged. "I haven't gotten back to them."

How considerate, I wanted to say but I shut my mouth. This was not the time to fly off the handle. I knew I wasn't thinking straight lately, especially today, I knew I was predisposed to say shit I didn't mean, hell, shit I didn't even think. I couldn't fuck everything up now, not when we were so close.

"Well, you can do whatever you want to do," I lied

through my teeth. "You're a free agent. We haven't signed anything."

Cuz I'm a dick-grabbing monkey, that's why.

My cell phone rang, preventing me from saying anything else ridiculous. It was Jenn but I was grateful for any distraction.

"Hey babe," I said.

"Dex?" Jenn's voice sounded tinny through the poor reception. "Sorry to bug you on your little adventure but Cynthia and Reece wanted to have a girl's night out and..."

She droned on but I had quit listening and was watching Perry again. Her nose twitched (how cute was that?) and a faint flush of red crept up her neck and onto the side of her face. She straightened up in her seat as soon as she noticed me looking but it didn't stop the girl from looking like she'd rather be in a million other places than sitting here in front of me. I hoped she wasn't seriously thinking about that pussy ghost hunting club. Who the fuck decides to form one of those?

"....and I know you won't be home till late, but I won't be there until probably much later. Is that OK?"

"Yeah, that's fine."

"You sure?" Jenn asked and from her tone I knew she didn't give a fuck if I said it wasn't. She'd still go out, as she always did. I didn't even know why she was calling to ask. Maybe she wanted to check up on me.

"Seriously, I don't mind. Go do whatever it is you girls do."

After I told her I'd be home in the morning now, I hung up the phone and decided to jump right back into it.

"OK, where were we?" I said out loud. What did we need to know for tonight?

"She doesn't mind you staying another night?" Perry asked.

I raised my brow. Odd question. Why did she care?

"No," I said, not wanting to talk about how pathetic our relationship truly was. I let my gaze fall to the window where the wind was shaking the trees loose. I breathed in and let that smell of home bring my heart rate down a notch.

"Do you have anymore pie?"

"There's a slice or two I put back in the fridge..." she said, as if she wasn't sure.

"Would you mind getting me a piece of pie?" I asked. I wanted to see if she'd do it. And if she'd hand it to me again with that look in her eyes. I needed that look right now. I sensed some changes inside, the wiring coming loose and needing a good cauterizing. My thoughts were getting lost.

She tried to look annoyed but she failed at it big time. Cuz she still got out of her chair and walked over to the fridge. She opened the door and had to bend over in front of me to get a bottle of milk. My god she had one hell of an ass. Not too big that your dick would get lost but just big enough to get a good, meaty hold and squeeze and smack and come until the cows came home.

I must have been pretty obvious in my leering. Wasn't I trying to impress her, not creep her out?

"Were you staring at my ass?" she said. She sounded surprised but she was glaring at me, so I had no idea what the fuck she was thinking. Did she like the idea? Was she going to tell her mafia uncle to pour cement in my shoes and chuck me out in the Pacific?

"Yes," I told her. Why lie? I'd put on the cement shoes if I had to. I've done worse for a woman.

She made some exasperated sound and shook her head.

But she still came back with a piece of pie. She was beet red now and avoiding my eyes. Maybe she liked my attention after all.

"Obviously, I'll need a napkin too," I told her. Pushing buttons, pushing buttons.

"Obviously," she muttered and she tossed one to me. I took it with all the grace of a dandy and folded it in my shirt pocket. I was a gentleman over everything. An ass-appreciating gentleman. We are the finest kind of man. I should open my own ass-appreciating gentleman's club one day.

I shoved the pie in my face (pie-appreciating gentleman that I am) and noticed she wasn't having any. To think of it, she hadn't had any earlier either. That's probably why I thought she baked it for me...she certainly didn't bake the dessert for herself.

Oh no, don't tell me she's one of those self-conscious girls who have absolutely no reason to be self-conscious. I eyed her full breasts and couldn't fathom why she'd want to diet.

"You're not having anything?" I asked, pointing my fork at her in an accusatory fashion, hoping she'd prove me wrong.

"I don't like pie," was her stupid answer.

I laughed and a piece of pie shot out. "You don't like pie? What kind of person doesn't like pie?"

I poked her with the fork to make sure she was still real. "You can't be trusted."

She took a swipe at the fork, looking annoyed. "You're the one with the fork."

Without thinking, I reached over for her hand and opened it, soft and warm. I placed the fork in it and gently closed her fingers over it.

"Now you have the fork," I said softly and sat back in

my chair. She stared down at the fork, thinking. I stared down at the paper. Thinking. Sometimes you came across women who had everything going for them...looks, personality, smarts, and they had NO fucking idea what they were worth. How amazing and beautiful they were, how they oozed sex and secrets. Then you had those women who knew they had what you wanted and used it. Repeatedly. Just to get what they wanted. It was an unbalanced universe.

Now I could see that Perry was the former. She did look self-conscious and unsure of herself at every turn. She was always pulling down her shirt or tugging up her jeans, or keeping her chin as far away from her neck as possible. She'd cover up her breasts with heavy jackets and boxy shirts, like they were something to be hidden. The girl was fucking nuts and for all the wrong reasons. It made me feel strangely helpless.

"I just want you to enjoy all the pies in life, Perry," I said, gazing at her, trying to get her shy eyes to meet mine. "That's all."

I wondered if she'd let me try.

FIVE
BIG DUMB SEX

It was nearly five in the morning when I finally pulled the car into the garage. I had been so close to taking out a few trees and road signs on the drive up from Portland that I started blaring shitty pop music with the windows down, just so the disgust and cold would keep me awake.

It worked. I didn't crash the car though as I staggered over to the elevator with my duffel bag in tow, I kinda wished I had. I had Rebecca Black in my head, a fate worse than death.

My plan was to enter the apartment as quietly as possible. If luck was on my side I'd be able to sneak inside without waking up Jenn and I could put off facing her until a reasonable hour, until I had ten cups of black coffee and a few sneaked cigarettes.

Lady Luck, that saucy bitch, was *not* on my side. As soon as my keys started to jangle in the hole, the door flung open and there she was. And, as I thought, she was ready to kill me.

Yeah, the thing is even though I spoke to her earlier in the day when I was at Perry's uncle's and told her I'd be coming home in the morning, even though she said she didn't care and that she was going out with her bimbo posse anyway, I knew she'd be mad. I just knew it. And I was right. I was always fucking right.

"Hey babe," I said quietly, trying to flash her a smile she once thought was charming.

She narrowed her eyes and didn't let me in.

"It's the middle of the night," she hissed.

"I can see that," I said and blinked at her hair. It was in a wild 'fro on top of her head, her face was without a lick of makeup. She did look gorgeous but she also looked evil. It was the heat seething from her eyes. "Are you going to let me in or shall I sleep out in the hall? There's a cozy spot in the stairwell, I discovered that the last time you –"

"Last time I what?" she asked carefully. She raised her chin and eyed me down.

Last time you got totally jealous because I was hanging around some girl. Even though it was Rebecca. Even though she's a lesbian.

"Last time we had disagreements," I said. I put my hand up on the door and pushed it in a few inches. "Please. Babe. I've had a rough day."

"Where the hell have you been?" she asked though she stepped away and let me in.

I walked in and tossed my bag on the couch.

"I told you earlier. You called *me,* remember?"

She folded her arms across her chest and tried to stifle a yawn. "I thought you'd wait until morning. Maybe have some respect for my beauty sleep. It's *Wine Babes*, not *Wine Hags*, you know."

Boy, did I ever.

"Perry had to get home, she works in the morning," I explained, my voice hesitating only slightly. I watched her reaction and wondered what ground I was treading on tonight.

Her eyes flashed like lightening, almost too quick to see. Then the mask of indifference slid on her features and she looked at me with a perfectly blank expression.

"Who is Perry?"

She wasn't fooling anyone but I let her play her game.

"You know, the girl with the lighthouse." As if Perry wasn't the sole reason Jenn had called me earlier.

"Girl?"

I shrugged. "Yeah, girl. She's like twenty or something."

White heat erupted from her gaze. I'd forgotten that the younger another woman was, the worse things got.

For me.

I sighed and turned away from my glowering girlfriend, ready for bed, ready to turn off my brain. I had bigger things to worry about than Jenn. I mean, fuck, the lighthouse actually fucking exploded. It exploded! I had nearly died tonight. We both nearly did and it would have been on my conscious if anything had happened to Perry. I spent the whole drive home trying not to think about it, trying not to think about what I thought I saw. What I couldn't have seen.

"Dex?" Jenn asked, her voice breaking into my thoughts before they foundered. I felt her hand on my shoulder, her grip firm and warm. "Are you OK?"

I turned my head slightly and spied her out of the corner of my eye.

"I'm just tired. It's nothing. I'm hitting the sack."

I started to step forward when her grip tightened on my shoulder and held me back.

"Dex," she said again, using my name in a deliberate way. There was warmth to it, enough to make me realize she was...what was this? Concern about me? My heart lurched around in my chest. Tricky little bastard.

I turned to face her and her hands immediately went to my waist. With hooded eyes she took her delicate, long fingers and started stroking back and forth along the waistband, teasing my skin.

I knew those moves all too well. Did she care or did she just want to get laid?

Fuck, why did I even bother thinking? I didn't care either.

The fear I felt turned to flames. The night turned to need. I needed to be distracted, from Perry, from ghosts, from death. As usual, this would do.

Oh, this would do all right.

With one hand she popped the button on my pants. She dropped to her knees. I got hard instantly, knowing what was coming next.

Me.

Out of all the women I'd been with, Jenn knew her blessed way around a cock. Sometimes I wondered if she'd been a man herself in a past lifetime. Not that I liked to think that when she was unzipping my fly with her teeth, but there was no question she was a woman who knew exactly what you needed and wanted and was never ashamed to give it to you.

Sexually, anyway.

The minute my cock came free of my pants, heavy and twitching with anticipation, I grabbed the back of her head with both my hands, making a tight fist in her hair and yanked her toward me. She gave a little moan from the pain and took all of me in her mouth, and then some. She expertly gripped me in a squeezing motion with one hand, and let her fingers play with my balls with the other.

In seconds, I didn't have a thought in my head, except that I wanted it harder, faster, more, more, more. Part of me wanted to come now and hard, the other part wanted to prolong the pleasure as long as possible. As selfish as it was, I didn't really care if she got off or not. This was about me, my need to forget, my need to only feel this dirty high. Jenn didn't really care either, she could always take care of herself. There were no tallies with us. We both always got what we wanted in the end.

She started to twirl her tongue along, rubbing it hard along the ridge. Fuck, I was going to lose it quickly if she kept that up.

Then she pulled away and wiped her mouth before grinning at me. If my mind wasn't so clouded by lust, I could have sworn she looked positively fake.

"How about you take me from behind?" she purred. Without waiting for me to respond, she slipped off her short shorts, her thin top, and she was bare ass naked. She flung herself down on the couch and arched her back invitingly.

Fuck me. I could never *ever* say no to that.

I guided myself in, grabbed her around the small of her itty, bitty waist and pushed in hard. She moaned some more, loudly...too loudly.

"Yes, fuck me harder Dex," she yelled.

I almost laughed. *Fuck me harder Dex?* Was she kidding? Now Jenn was always delightfully nasty and vocal at times, but it sounded like she was trying a little too hard. It sounded scripted.

I slowed the thrusting down and tried to get my mind back on track. Who cares if she was putting on a show, I was getting laid, wasn't I? My dick was full-up inside her, what was the problem? No problem.

"You're so good," she cried out again in a breathy voice.

I bit my lip. What the hell was she doing? I liked porn but I liked it realistic and raw, not cheap and tawdry and that's exactly what she was acting like. For the first time ever she was acting like someone else, someone...insecure.

Then it hit me. This was about Perry, wasn't it? Oh of course it was. I was a fucking idiot for not seeing it.

Naturally, I was turned on, inside her to the hilt and my load was threatening to blow at any minute, so her cheesy porn star act and insecurities weren't enough to make me stop or distract me. But the thought of Perry herself, well, that was distracting.

And pleasantly so.

I moved my hands down to Jenn's tight ass, increased my speed, and closed my eyes. No one could complain about Jenn's body, but I wondered what it would be like to have Perry on all fours in front of me. If it was her I was fucking, with that big, gorgeous ass of hers, I'd have a lot more under my hands, soft flesh I could squeeze and knead and lick and bite. I wondered if she'd like it from behind, if she'd moan with every inch of me. I wondered if she'd let me grab her thick, dark mane and hold it like a pair of reins, if I could make her come with my girth alone or if I'd need to reach down and stroke her until she literally dripped on the carpet.

Fuck.

I came hard.

The hardest in a long time. I dug my fingers into Jenn's ass, causing her to give a legitimate whimper of pain, and bit my tongue to stop me from screaming out Perry's name. My legs shook as the deluge pumped into Jenn in endless, brain-seizing waves. I couldn't stop seeing Perry's face, someone so innocent that needed to be defiled. Someone who might possibly need me to show her some things for a change.

When I was finished, I pulled out of Jenn and walked to the bathroom, feeling dizzy, my heart firing at a million beats a minute. I heard her cry out in indignation at something or other, but it didn't matter. I went in and closed the door behind me and leaned against the sink.

What the fuck is wrong with me? I thought.

I just got off thinking about Perry, my 22-year-old potential partner, and it was the best orgasm I'd had in months. Years.

I wiped the sweat off my brow and looked at myself in the mirror.

You, sir, are asking for trouble.

I closed my eyes to my flushed reflection and bright, dilated pupils. Immediately an image of Perry sprung up on my head again, this time she was on her back, lying beneath me, her breasts rising, anticipating me.

I quickly locked the bathroom door and stroked myself at the thought.

I came again and right away.

Fuck trouble. I wasn't asking for it.

I was inviting it.

SIX

BUTTERFLY CAUGHT

"So have you made love to her yet?"

I shot Maximus a look. "Made love to her? What the fuck is wrong with you dude, it's not the '50s."

He shrugged and kept a stupid smile on his lips while turning his attention back to the desert. His flaming red hair matched the dust that blew past the jeep.

"Anyway," I said, trying not to grip the wheel too hard, "and not that it's any of your damn business, but no. I have not *made love* to her. Nor have I fucked her. We're just partners."

"Good," he said. I didn't like his tone. It sounded like he was patting me on the back or something. Fuck that. It seemed ever since Max randomly stepped back into my life in Red Fox, every second with him was rubbing me the wrong way. Apparently, I still had an axe to grind and if I didn't know any better, he had one to grind with me. He was just hiding it behind his stupid drawl and fake air of decency.

I bit my lip until I tasted blood. With no meds in my body, I felt royally screwed up and I was constantly battling the urge to act up and out. What I really wanted to do was pull the car over to the side of the road, tell him if he wanted to keep his dick attached, he needed to stay far away from Perry. Then I'd kick him out and make him walk to the ranch. Perhaps he'd get eaten by a coyote while he was out there.

Wishful thinking. Deranged, but wishful thinking.

He gave me a sly look out of the corner of his eye.

"What?" I asked testily.

He shrugged again. My grip tightened. I wanted out of the car. Why did we have to go all the way into town to do the atmospheric shots? It was too damn hot and I couldn't spend another moment in this inferno with him. All his red hair just fanned the heat.

When he didn't say anything, I flipped on the stereo, letting the Deftones distract me. Unfortunately angry music doesn't help an already angry guy.

"She's cute, you know," he commented, his voice raised over the music.

"Yeah, so?"

His shoulders lifted up.

"Don't you dare fucking shrug again!"

He smiled and looked down at his all too clean fingernails.

"I'm just saying, she's cute. I'm surprised you haven't made a move on her," he said. Then he added under his breath, "Since you make a move on pretty much every woman you come across."

Ah, here was the axe. Grind, grind, grind.

I cleared my throat. My god I needed water. Or a beer. Or a bottle of bourbon with a bucket of ice. It felt like I swallowed the contents of a vacuum bag.

"I have respect for Perry, believe it or not," I told him.

He chuckled to himself. "Right. I'm gonna guess you already tried to put the moves on her and the little lady turned you down? What did you do, the good ol' Dex Foray special, tried to put your Johnson up her ass?"

"What the hell is wrong with you?" I countered. "I did no such thing, and you know that's not the Dex Foray special. The Dex Foray special involves two lubed fingers, a lot of tongue and a cigarette for afterwards."

Speaking of cigarette. I fished one out of my pocket and lit it with one hand.

"Do you mind if I smoke?" I asked not caring what his answer was.

"Yes."

"Didn't you used to smoke?" I brought the cigarette to my lips and inhaled. I blew the smoke out at him and grinned.

He coughed and waved at me, annoyed. Good. "I used to do a lot of things Dex."

"So where you been keeping yourself all these years?"

"I already told you. Nice way to change the subject. You're still the king of that."

"Better than thinking I am *the* king. When you going to get rid of the Elvis do, Max? Guess that's a thing you still do. You know, look like a douchebag."

"Funny," he remarked. "Same insults."

"I'm the same boy, Max. So are you."

"I'm not. And it's Maximus," he shot out. He looked back to the dry scenery flying past, the hills of stark rock and dark chasms. In the distance lay the ranch. We had arrived, thank god.

Just as we were pulling up to the Lancaster's house, Max had to get one last thing in.

"So is she single?"

I slammed the jeep into park. "Who?"

"Oh, you know. Perry. The little lady with the...nice endowments."

I wanted to wipe the shit-eating grin off of his freckled face. I couldn't even answer. If I said no, I'd be lying. If I said yes, he'd start going for her. And given the weird way I felt about Perry and the even weirder history I had with Max, that was one hell of a bad fucking idea.

So I didn't say anything. I just shot him a dirty look and hoped to god he didn't round up the courage to start hitting on her. He had a strange sense of confidence though. I guess being built like a small giant had its advantages. Chicks always fell for it. I had to rely on my good looks and goddamn charm.

We walked back to the house, me leading the way. The sad sack that was Will was standing at the foot of the front steps, his dark eyes searching the rugged horizon of his ranch.

"Hey Will," I said. I stopped beside him in the dry dust and tried to follow his gaze. "Whatcha looking at?"

"Bird," he replied absently.

"Fair enough."

I left him in the desert and went with Max inside. It was wonderfully cool in the house, though I'm sure having a frigid bitch like Sarah as a wife probably had something to do with it. I went straight for the couch and flopped down on it. Sure, I was a guest here and it was probably rude to just put my sweaty body on their furniture, but whatever. It's hot out. Deal with it.

After a few seconds, I realized the frigid bitch herself was sitting on the chair across from me. She was staring right at me. I mean, she had those damn shades on so I couldn't see her eyes, but I could feel them. Blind as a bat and I could swear she was watching me. That and sucking the thoughts out of my brain. I shivered despite the heat.

"So, where's Perry?" I asked, wanting to make some conversation. I knew she was probably upstairs in our room anyway. I had an image of her reeling from the heat, lying down on our bed in next to nothing. Crap. I really hoped Sarah was blind because she did not need to see the rise in my pants.

"She's gone. Missing. Bird has gone looking for her," she told me calmly.

My head snapped up. "What?"

"You heard me. You really ought to keep your wife under control. She's becoming a nuisance."

I heard her, barely. I got to my feet, shoving down the panic that was building up in my chest, and ran for the door. Max, who was nearby in the kitchen (always fucking nearby) followed behind me.

I flung myself down the steps to say something to Will when out in the distance I saw Bird and Perry walking together. Well, Bird was walking. Perry was limping. She looked like she'd fallen off a cliff.

She was alive, which was a plus. But she was hurt and I had a feeling it was all because she didn't fucking listen to me.

Fuck. I was mad. Mad? I was livid.

Whatever anger I felt earlier because of Max, it was coming out now and there was nothing I could do to stop it. I let my emotions run wild and ran up to her, throwing my hands in the air.

"What the fuck happened to you?"

She looked scared at my reaction but I didn't care.

Bird gave me a sympathetic bullshit smile. "She took a little tumble, she's fine."

"She's not fine," I spat out, struggling to keep my voice down.

She was scraped from head to toe with a giant bloody gash at her cheek. Her tank top was ripped and bloodied and she was barely standing up straight. I'd never felt such an intense rush of anger and sorrow before. I wanted to yell at her, then take her under my wing and make sure nothing like this ever happened to her again.

Bird knew when to leave. "I'll go get the first aid kit."

I gave him a look and then turned back to Perry. Looking at her was breaking my heart into a million pieces. I wanted to hurt the bastard who did this to her and it was hard knowing there was no one to blame except Perry.

"I'm sorry," she said. "It's no big deal."

I anxiously rubbed at my chin, feeling too much and having nowhere to put it.

"What happened?"

She explained. It didn't help. First there was going off and walking by herself when I told her to stay put. I wasn't saying those things to be a dick, I said it because I knew she attracted danger and, goddamn it, I cared about her. Then she had to literally fall off a cliff, get attacked by a crow and almost get bitten by a snake before Bird annihilated it with a gun. The results of that were all over her shirt in sticky patches.

"Well I hate to say I told you so, but, I so fucking told you so," I said. "You want to listen to me next time?"

She didn't look ashamed in the slightest. I guess I was putting her on the defensive, as usual.

"It depends, Dex," she said with a glare, giving my name special hated emphasis. "You're not normally the voice of reason here."

True.

"Neither of us is. You better wash up."

We went back into the house. I watched Maximus's eyes seeing if he was dumb enough to lay the Southern charm on but he looked mildly horrified and only offered up "my lord" as we passed by.

Perry went up the stairs to the room and the minute she shut the door behind her, I turned to her Bird who was coming out of the kitchen with a first aid kit in his hands.

"What the hell, Bird?" I yelled.

"Easy, Dex," Max said.

"Oh shut the fuck up," I told him without a glance. I snatched the kit out of Bird's worn hands. "Why did you let her go off like that?"

Bird put that oh-so-wise and patient look on his face, his lines growing deeper. He didn't say anything for a few seconds and calmly folded his arms. Those eyes of his had a very calming effect on me.

Finally he said, "I did not know she had left. As soon as I found out she had, I followed her tracks into the mountain. I arrived...just in time."

He let those last words sink in a little. AKA you should thank me you white asshole.

I shot him a weak but appreciative smile. "Well, thanks then. I just..."

Bird nudged me and gestured to the ceiling. "Go tend to your wife. She needs you."

I nodded, hoping my face wasn't portraying the sudden heat I felt at the mention of "wife" and went up the stairs.

She was in the bathroom but I didn't hear the shower running.

I gave a quick rap on the door.

"It's Dex," I said giving her enough time to cover

herself. I tried the handle. Locked. Guess she thought I was the type of guy who would ambush her in the shower.

Guess she was kind of right about that.

The door eventually opened a crack and Perry gave me a suspicious look. That's all I noticed before I spied her breasts which were spilling over the top of her towel. And by towel, I mean dishcloth. The girl was dangerously close to having a nipple slip.

"Hello there," I said in an extremely sleazy voice. Didn't mean to, just slipped out. I hoped her breast might follow suit.

"How long have you been standing there?" I heard her ask. She sounded far away. All I could see was skin and cleavage and beads of water rolling down full mounds and...

She reached over and pushed at my forehead until my eyes were forced to meet hers. That was OK. I liked staring into her eyes as much as I liked staring at her boobs.

"Did you just see Sarah leave?" she asked, tension in her voice.

"Why?" I looked at her closely. She looked more scared than annoyed at my leering, and when my head cleared of the blatant sexuality on display, I remembered why I had come up there. Her pale skin was marred with rough, red scratches up and down her arms, on her hands, her face.

She closed her eyes and sighed, getting ready to close the door. "Nevermind."

I quickly put my arm up to stop it. "Nuh uh." I pushed my way into the bathroom and shut the door behind me. "You need some attending."

"Oh yeah, you'd like that wouldn't you?" she sniped and took a step back from me.

Sheesh. What the hell was her problem? I wasn't the one who told her to go off into the desert with her arms wide open yelling "Come to me my animal friends!" I told her to do the opposite.

I raised my brow at her in warning. Then I sighed, opened the kit up in the sink and said, "Actually I'd like it if you were being the sexy nurse, not me."

I tried not to imagine that hot little fantasy of mine and concentrated on the task at hand—pouring alcohol on gauze and cleaning up her wounds. Time to man up and quit thinking with my dick.

She flinched as I pressed the solution into her arm but she held it together for the most part. I have to admit, it was a bit unnerving being so close to her when she had on just a towel. Hell, if I was being honest here, it's unnerving being close to her in general. The way she smelled, the feel of her skin beneath my hands, it was intoxicating. And confusing.

And there I was with my dick thinking again. Although...it wasn't just that. And that was the confusing part, wasn't it?

Fuck, forgetting my pills was a bad, bad choice.

I rerouted my brain and concentrated on getting her better. When I was done wrapping her hands with a shit-load of gauze, I met her eyes. We had a moment. I tried to read her. There was too much going on inside both of us for me to get a clear picture.

"I'm sort of waiting for you to tell me how this happened," I said softly. "I mean, not the *CliffsNotes* version of things."

Now she looked embarrassed. She took in a deep breath and explained everything down to the dream she had before she even came to Red Fox. Now that pissed me off. I know that we barely knew each other and we were just partners when it came down to things but, I don't know, I felt strangely betrayed that she hadn't confided in me about it. It was like she didn't trust me with things for fear of what I would think. That would have been flattering if it wasn't a little off-putting. I wanted her to trust me but it was apparent it would be slow going.

When she finished telling me how the crow attacked her and how lucky she was for Bird to have showed up (luck didn't even begin to cover it), I was pretty much done. All I had to do was clean the cut on her cheek.

"You know the drill," I told her. I touched her face with my hands and leaned in closer. My eyes tried to stay focused on the wound but it was hard. I wanted to look into her eyes at this close of a distance. I wanted to let her know she was going to be OK. There was something so vulnerable and restrained about Perry, something that made me want to do stupid, ridiculous things to keep her safe. At the same time, I wanted to draw her out and make her strong, like a diamond from coal.

Without even realizing it, I found myself gazing deep into those blue eyes, totally fucking lost in them. My heart did a little flip. Christ, this was not a good idea. My heart of all hearts did not need to be flipping.

I broke away, broke the tension, broke the connection, and gave her one final dab of iodine on her cheek. I gave her a forced smile, already feeling distant. Distance was good.

"You're going to have a rusty blotch on your face from the iodine, but I think if you wash it in an hour you should be good to go."

"Thanks Dex," she said, her voice barely above a whisper. She looked away, staring absently at the sink. She felt the distance too. This was for the best.

For now.

SEVEN

SHE'S GOT A WAY

"Sexually frustrated?" Perry asked, her voice struggling to be heard in the noisy bar.

I turned my head away from my beer bottle and looked at her in surprise. The girl must have been psychic, though I could see from the way her round eyes were slanting at the corners that she might just be drunk.

I had to smile. "Yes."

There was really no use in denying it. Even with all the bullshit going around and the feeling that my brain was splitting in two, it was having to sleep next to her every night – and just sleep – that was fucking me up the most. I looked down at the beer bottle label that was sticking to my fingers in moist chunks. Christ, I couldn't be more obvious.

She didn't appear put-off. She rarely did. It was one of her annoying superpowers.

"Because your girlfriend isn't here?"

"Sure." That was part of it. But even if Jenn were here, god help us all, it still wouldn't have gotten rid of the constant boner adjustments.

I took a long gulp of my beer, hoping that she would get

the hint and not pry any further. Perry didn't seem to have control over her lips half the time and not in a good way and it was only a matter of time before I said something really stupid. I didn't trust myself without the meds.

I glanced up at Maximus and Bird talking across the table from us. I hated Max again. I didn't know if it was being off the meds or whatthefuckever but his rockabilly bullshit act was wearing thin. I didn't like how he acted like he knew everything and I didn't like the way he was trying to win Perry over. He would deny it, but I knew exactly what the fucker was trying to do to me. And Perry was too innocent, her self-esteem too ravaged to pick up on it.

To cement my point, Dire Straits came on and after Perry proclaimed her sudden (and surprising) love for the band, the douchefucker stood up and asked her to dance like he was a Cajun Rhett Butler.

She agreed, taking his hand with a look that was pretty close to glee, and he led her to the packed dance floor. I looked back at the beer just in case she wanted me to notice what was going on, notice them together. My fingers started picking at the label again. I wouldn't give them that satisfaction.

"You care about her a great deal," Bird said in his 'I'm an old man' voice.

I shot him a look and resumed concentration on the beer, taking respite in the monotonous movements. I didn't say anything. There wasn't anything to say. It was the truth, that's all it was.

"It's OK, Dex," he continued. "I would too. But you have to respect each other. You have to move slowly. You are both too much the same."

"What does that mean?" I snapped at him. I felt bad,

once again I wasn't in control of my emotions, but Bird's face was impassive and gave nothing away.

"You know what it means," he said, and he left it at that. I did know what he meant. That's what made the whole situation harder.

We sat in silence for a bit, then he excused himself to go to the bar, promising to bring me a beer. I wanted to stick my fucking head in a pitcher but I needed to take it easy. Drinking never really helped me in the way I thought it did. And those thoughts always came when I was three sheets to the wind.

I managed to avoid looking in Max and Perry's direction but that all went fuckaloo when U2 came on and Perry wasn't back at her seat with fingers in her ears.

Instead she was still on the dance floor. Slow dancing. With ginger fucking Elvis. They were dancing close, way too close. Her breasts were crammed up into his chest, he was holding her like he was about to turn her over his knee and spank her six ways from Sunday.

And she was letting him. She looked like she was enjoying the body pressure as much as he was. I could only imagine the way his chubby must have been grinding against her. Not that I wanted to imagine that. I shuddered, feeling the curious mix of disgust and envy carry through me. Feelings, fuck, I wasn't used to this.

I was still making a disgusted face when Bird came back, but to his credit he just handed me my beer and didn't say anything. It was taking all my willpower to peel my eyes away from the couple and concentrate on something else.

This came in the form of Cheri and Amanda, two MILFs who had been eyeing me since I sat down. I'm sure they probably went after any guy under thirty-five who didn't clean his ears out with his car keys, but I decided to be flattered. I grinned at them and as expected they teetered over to me on tacky plastic heels, smiles broad, breaths rank.

I didn't really hear a word they were saying, I was just trying to look handsome and not breathe in through my nose. One of them, Cheri, maybe, took a liking to Bird, which he didn't seem to mind. Bird didn't strike me as someone who had a wife waiting for him at home, though he could have certainly done better than some old lush with wrinkled cleavage and brown-speckled teeth. I felt like throwing up in my mouth but I played up my virility and asked Amanda, maybe, if she'd help choose songs from the jukebox with me.

We walked to the box through the sticky crowd and I kept Perry and Max in my peripheral vision. On the outside it looked like I was having fun, on the inside I was paranoid as fuck. I kept fearing that he'd grab her and take her away somewhere dark and private. The thought of him touching her, kissing her, bothered me to no end but Amanda was watching me and looking confused at my expression. I smiled at her again, all good vibes and good sex, and let her select some shitty songs first before I requested mine.

We had just gotten back to the table (where Bird was trying to give Cheri a very polite GTFO) when Max and Perry finally removed themselves from the floor. I wanted to make some cutting remark to him and cut him down a peg but there was a weird aura of tension just steaming off. Something had gone down between them and even though it soothed the spite in me, I was a bit concerned for Perry.

Apparently, so was Amanda. The minute she saw Perry's sweet, worried face she grabbed my arm, sinking her Pepto Bismol–colored talons into my skin.

"You're dancing with me, sugar," she commanded. She

was surprisingly strong for her size and her sun-leathered arms had no problem dragging me to my feet.

"Like I have a choice," I said, trying not to laugh. This was one hungry cougar.

I gave Perry a quick wink as we went past and decided to give Amanda what she'd been waiting for: Someone young. Someone fun. I grabbed a cowboy hat off of some random Joe Blow and gave "Crocodile Rock" my best moves.

It had been a while since I was able to use some of my theatre school skills, other than fucking Michelle in the orchestra pit and taking hits between monologues. I knew it didn't matter if I screwed up or looked like a fool because that wasn't the point, but I was surprised how easily it came back to me. Again, all I could think about was how deep I felt the music, how deep I was feeling...everything. Though I was swinging Amanda around, my mind dwelled on what my medication was hiding half the time. Besides the very obvious.

"You're good," Amanda said to me, holding me close to her, trying to take back the control. People were clapping and watching us with amusement and she was basking in the glow.

"It comes naturally. But so does being bad," I said with a smirk.

"I can see that. Your wife must be pretty pissed."

Wife? Oh right. Fuckity fuck. I didn't need to eye the ring on my finger to remember the whole charade. Not that the town of Red Fox gave two shits whether I was really married to Perry or pretend married, but it didn't hurt to keep up appearances.

"She's pretty understanding," I said.

Amanda nodded. I noticed her earrings were clip-ons

and dangerously close to slipping off. This was one sweaty, stanky-ass bar.

"You're the understanding one. Most men here would be all macho about it if their wife was dancing with another man. But I could see he wasn't a threat at all."

Oh really? I wanted to pry her for her cougarly wisdom but I bit my lip instead. We danced some more and then we were interrupted by another woman. She said her name was Mary Sue (naturally) and she was years younger (possibly even underage) with desperate eyes that screamed at me, like dancing with Dex Foray was the most excitement she'd ever get. That made me really fucking sad. How pathetic this town must be to find a fuck-up like me as their savior.

I danced with Mary Sue, going through the motions, thinking about the fake wedding band on my ring finger. When the song ended again and I could see more women approaching me (look, I get that I can look pretty hot, but no one should attract this many barflies), I decided I had enough. I knew what song was next and I knew who I was dancing with. My wife.

I walked toward her, ignoring the women and focused on her face until her big blue eyes met mine. She looked so small and dainty sitting there among Max and Bird, drinking and trying to have fun even though a world of danger whirled around her. I could see the strain on her face. I knew she was always hyper-aware of what lurked in the dark. I knew because Bird was right. We were too much the same.

I stopped in front of her and tipped my hat in the most awkward imitation of a cowboy.

"It's our song," I said to her over the piano notes of Billy Joel's "She's Always a Woman." I held out my hand, hoping she'd take it.

Her eyes lit up and she took my hand. I quickly grasped it, cool and white between my fingers. I led her to the floor and put my arm around her, bringing her in hard and fast to my side. She was mine. For the sake of appearances, she was my wife, but she was mine anyway. She didn't know it yet, but I did. It was wrong and it made no sense, but she belonged with me. No one else, not anyone else.

It was a shame that I was the one who belonged to someone else. I wondered if I'd ever have the strength to correct that or if I'd punish myself forever.

We started dancing slowly, side to side, and I put one hand behind her back, where it was hot and small, temptingly close to her ass. The other held her hand. I kept her as close to me as possible, but I didn't want to impose like Maximus did. Besides, the last thing Perry needed was to feel my hard-on on her hip, even though it was fucking tempting to let her know what she was doing to me. I entertained the idea that she might even like it. It was a high school dance all over again.

I had to know. I stared into her eyes, lost in the storm, and started singing along with Joel. Softly, and at a distance to start, then I leaned into her ear where it smelled like sunshine and baby powder. I closed my eyes and sang, feeling my breath bound off of her ear in hot clouds. It was taking all of my willpower to not take this further, to not wrap my lips around it and lick the lobe to see what it would taste like. See if I could make those eyes roll back and make her forget everything that had happened to her. I didn't want to be Red Fox's savior, but I wanted to be hers.

As if hearing my thoughts and welcoming them, she laid her head on my shoulder. I tried willing my heart to beat slower, knowing how fast it was racing now. This felt so perfect, a perfection I didn't deserve but I would take it if I could get it.

And then *wham bam thank you ma'am* the spell was gone. Perry raised her head back and looked wide-eyed and vaguely frightened. I couldn't figure her out if I tried. But I wouldn't let her go. The song ended, but I kept my arms wrapped tight around her, not letting her move an inch. If she was having some internal battle again, she could do so in my arms.

"Whatcha doing, wifey?" I joked, secretly enjoying the sound of that.

She gave me a look of forced casualness. "Song's over."

Right. Like that's what happened behind those deep eyes of hers.

"Is it?" I asked, knowing exactly what was coming next. Yep, I was a smooth one tonight. Found two Billy Joel songs on the jukebox and bogarted them both. I was sure the hillbilly folks of Red Fox would be put out without their country bullshit, but I was in town and I had a fake wife to impress.

I don't know if she was impressed, though. She looked shocked. I didn't know if that was good or bad.

"Don't look so worried," I told her, trying to put her at ease. "Best fifty cents I ever spent."

"What, did you select Billy Joel's *Greatest Hits* or something?"

Er, maybe she wasn't finding it as charming as I thought. Maybe I was being creepy. Wouldn't be the first time.

"Well, I tried," I admitted. "But these were the only two songs. I'm afraid it's Poison after this, so you should probably enjoy this dance while you can."

"You really like Billy Joel, don't you?"

Oh, she was just so clueless. Bless her heart. I brought

her in closer to me so she'd start picking up on the right idea, which was the wrong idea. Or a bad, naughty idea.

"He's all right," I said, having a hard time keeping my amused grin under wraps. "But I figured you might dance with me if I put this on. Only fair that I get to dance with my wife."

She blushed at my choice of words. "A good wife would dance with you to anything. Especially with you. You're a modern-day Gene Kelly."

Now it was my time to blush. Except that I'm a man and I don't do that.

I laughed instead. "Years of theatre school and that's the only thing that sticks."

It was true too. I was a pretty fucking good dancer before I got sucked into the film side of things. Though I gotta say, the tail I got in theatre school was one of the reasons I stuck around for so long.

Her eyes widened. She smiled, her breath hot and sweet. "You're going to continue to surprise me, aren't you?"

"I hope so," I said. "The element of surprise is all I have."

And to make my point, I did something I had wanted to do all night.

I reached down and took a firm grab of her sweet ass. It molded like soft putty in my hand.

I looked over to Maximus, hoping the twatwaffle was watching.

He was. He looked surprised. Bothered. Red brows knitted together.

I grinned at him and gave him the thumbs up.

Suck on that, Max.

"What the hell, Dex?" she whispered harshly.

Oh right, I still had her ass in my hand. I let go and put my hand at the small of her back. Still in reach.

"What?" I asked innocently. "I'm allowed to grab my wife's ass. She's got a nice one."

A strange look came over her eyes, like clouds from an incoming storm.

"What would Jennifer think?"

Oh, fuck man. Why did she have to go and ruin a perfectly good – and innocent, I might add – ass-grabbing moment like that? Jennifer. What the hell did she have to do with anything? This was about me and her. This was about now. Why couldn't she have left it like that?

Reality bites.

"There is no Jennifer in this scenario," I told her.

"You're skirting dangerous territory, Dex," she warned.

It's too bad that was the best territory to be in. What a little buzzkill I had in my hands.

"What do you mean?" I wanted to hear her say it.

She thought about it. She knew I was baiting her.

"Your girlfriend is awfully trusting of you, that's all."

It wasn't all. But it was right.

"We have a relationship based on trust. Just like you and I do."

The trust that I wasn't going to do anything to jeopardize either relationship unless I had a damn good reason. And, well, I hadn't seen the reason yet. It needed to be foolproof.

Oh, I had no fucking idea what I was thinking about. All booze plus no meds makes Dex a crazy boy.

I felt eyes watching my every move so I looked away from her sweet face and scanned the bar. There were two idiots in their twenties sitting nearby, staring intently at Perry. It gave me a very bad feeling. First of all, one of them looked like he got chewed up by a lawnmower and hastily put back together. The other was just dripping with Perry lust. It was a little nauseating. Fuck, I hoped I didn't look like that.

"Looks like you're attracting some yokels at ten o' clock," I told her, trying to sound breezy but wanting her to know it wasn't something flattering.

She observed them for a moment. They never broke their stare, even though now I was full-on giving them the Dex Foray glare.

She looked back to me and I softened my face.

"Lovely pair," she joked. "Are you suggesting I go for them?"

I twirled her around. "Only if you want to add another cut to that cheek."

We danced for a little bit more until the song ended and then I regretfully took my hands off of Perry and left her to go to the bathroom. It had felt so good to be holding her but it was back to reality and the tawdry, beer-soaked morons of Red Fox.

When I was done, I came back to the table where Maximus and Bird were talking. Max's head snapped up the moment he heard me approaching and the look in his eyes was brilliant. As in, he was still annoyed about the ass-grabbing move. Well good. Her ass wasn't technically mine to grab (not in the real world) but it sure as hell wasn't his either.

Perry wasn't at the table but I didn't want to ask where she was in case Maximus had some stupid answer. So I just slid in the seat beside him and started talking to Bird about the history of the town. Not that I hadn't learned quite a bit all ready, but I liked Bird, and Bird seemed more relaxed when he was talking about boring shit.

I don't know how much time had passed before it was apparent that Perry wasn't coming back anytime soon. Max had gotten up to go somewhere, so I asked Bird.

"Where's Perry?"

He looked over at the crowd, his stern eyes scanning every person.

"I don't know....she-"

I didn't hear what he said. The slight spark of panic in his eyes was enough for me to jump to my feet. I marched to the edge of the dance floor and tried to pick her out there. Then I went around the bar area, searching every table and booth. I went to the bar, still as packed with stanky people as ever, and then I went to the washrooms, hanging around the woman's one for a few minutes before I had this terrible, ball-grabbing sensation that she was in major trouble.

I hoped my instincts were wrong but when it came to Perry they never were. It was like I had some sort of, I don't know, it sounds lame to say *connection*, but that's kind of what it was.

I ran away from the washrooms and pushed my way through the crowd to the front door. Outside people were smoking, puking, making out. Perry wasn't one of them.

"Fuck," I swore under my breath and went back inside, the wall of sweat and heat hitting me like a bum paddle.

When I looked around again, I noticed the two yokels I spotted ogling her earlier were gone. Again, my balls seized. This was not good.

Not good, not good, not good, not good.

I spied an exit sign at the back and another door and scrambled my way through the crowd. At one point my borrowed cowboy hat fell off but I wasn't about to retrieve it.

I burst through the back doors and into the still of the

night, the sounds of the bar fading as the door closed behind me.

But, fuck.

Wait.

I heard noises coming from around the side of a truck.

I saw. Oh god. I saw feet sticking out. Perry's worn and dusty shoes.

My heart lurched, anger pulsing through my veins at the speed of light. It was a violent feeling. I shut down to everything except swift justice.

I couldn't even think. I walked slowly toward the back of the truck. I spotted a shovel in the back of the truck with some farm equipment and quickly yanked it out. The scraping noise of metal on metal was a dead giveaway so I had two seconds to act.

I leaped around the corner and brought the shovel down like I was batting a home run. It connected with the face of the ugly bastard and he went flying backward.

It was only then that I saw Perry underneath him, blood on her hands, life in her eyes.

"Perry!" I screamed. I went for her, falling to my knees beside her. I put my hands to her cheek, seeing how hurt she was. She was still clothed, but from the way her pants were unzipped, the way her stomach was bloodied...

I could barely choke out the words, "Are you hurt?"

She shook her head. At least there was that. I slipped my arms underneath her and brought her gently to her feet.

"I got you," I whispered. Then I remembered the other dude at the bar. "Was it just this guy?"

She didn't say anything but she didn't need to. I heard the crunch of gravel and saw her eyes go circle-wide. I turned on my heel, without thinking, without planning, and swung the shovel at my target.

And there I found the other guy, his face underneath my shovel as it connected with a sick crack and he went flying backward onto the ground.

I don't really remember what happened next. Something in me, something I tried to keep buried and starving, it came out. It overrode my entire body and all I could think about was wanting to, needing to, kill this man. This beast. This animal. I wanted to rip his heart out and eat it in front of him for what they did to my Perry.

I didn't rip out his heart but this got pretty ugly with the shovel there. It was only Perry's cry, her protest for me to stop, that made me realize there was no use. He was down. She's the one who needed me.

I dropped the shovel and ran to her. She was barely staying up right and her eyes were closing in lid-fluttering daze. I was losing her.

"Perry! Hang in there!" I yelled, holding her up. She went completely slack in my arms. I hoisted her above my shoulder, finding the strength deep inside (she was small but, fuck, boobs weigh a lot) and brought her to the door.

Just then, Bird came rushing out with Max and Rudy, a flashlight in his hand.

One look at Perry and the guys on the ground and they knew what to do.

I was ushered through the crowd toward Rudy's office.

We did get a lot of looks from the drunk patrons, but none of concern. Just curiosity. It made me wonder if hauling bleeding women around was a part of their nightly scene. It wouldn't have surprised me.

Luckily, being a medicine man wasn't the naïve stereotype I thought it was, using flowers and hocus pocus to heal people. He had syringes, vials, antibiotics and a whole mess of clinical stuff under his desk.

He cleared it off and I laid her down on top of it. He lifted up her shirt. The wound near her belly-button...it made my skin crawl. It made that beast want to come out of me again.

I spent the next hour trying to keep the rage under control. A police officer showed up and I had Maximus show them to where the two guys were. I couldn't go myself. I would have finished the job. They deserved death but I knew better than to give it to them.

When Perry was finally patched up, we took her still unconscious body to the jeep and gently placed her inside. I had hoped the rolling movement and noise of the car would have woken her up, but whatever she was drugged with (Rudy said she exhibited all the signs) was far too powerful. She was there but not there. I wanted all of her to be there. I wanted her to be awake and know she was OK. I had her.

We brought her into the house where Will immediately started fussing and flipping out. Everyone was on edge, angry, wanting answers and justice. So was I, but I had to take care of her first.

I brought her up to the bedroom, alone. I was about to put her on the bed when she started making noises. Gurgling noises. Puking noises.

There wasn't enough time. I made it as far as the bathroom with her before she puked up on herself. Trying to ignore the smell, I took her over to the toilet – she was walking a little now, but not talking – and held back her hair as she brought up the rest of the night.

When she was finally done, weak and dirty, I ran a bath for her, lukewarm. I took off her clothes and there was Perry below me, naked. She looked as vulnerable as a baby bird.

I gently put her in the bath and quickly bathed her myself, sponging her with a soapy shower puff, trying not to get her bandages wet. Her pajamas were next. She was now coherent enough to help me by putting her arms through the sleeves. Bird was now in the room with us, a shotgun in his hand. It didn't make me feel all that better. It felt like the damage was done.

I scooped her up in my hands and lowered her into the bed. Her eyes opened wider, taking me in for the first time in hours. There was a flash of horror as she regained memory of the night. Then there was something else. Something reserved especially for me.

Maybe it was a thank you.

Maybe it was something more.

It didn't matter. She was looking at me in a way I'd always dreamed. It's too bad I had to save her in order to get it.

I'd never stop saving her.

EIGHT
STRIPSEARCH

"WHERE ARE WE GOING?" PERRY ASKED FROM BESIDE me, taking in the sights of the city. They weren't too pretty at the moment. Granville Street was Vancouver's entertainment district, which meant street punks with suspiciously acquired dogs, pushy homeless people, jonesing drug addicts and stumbling, drunken idiots in Tap-Out shirts. Not to mention the Canucks had just won the hockey game against the Rangers, so everything was multiplied by a billion beers and douchebags.

I didn't want to tell her where we were going. If she knew, she'd back out. I was on a mission to expose her to my world and let her hair down a little bit. I felt like a king earlier when I convinced her to wear the Canucks jersey I bought. It looked so fucking hot on Perry, barely fitting over her breasts, and it was taking all of my willpower to stop me from ripping her jeans off and bending her over in the hotel room. In the bathroom. Anywhere would have done. I was getting hard again just thinking about it.

So, naturally, I decided to take her to a strip club. Fuck, the way I figured it, she needed to loosen up a little. Let her hair down, like I said. And if I walked around with an erection in there, no one would be the wiser. At least she wouldn't think it was attributed to her, which 90% of the time it was.

And honestly, I needed the distraction like nothing else. After the news from Jenn...my mind was in dire need of shutting down. It couldn't happen fast enough. There was no way in hell I could deal with that shit this weekend of all weekends. Call me a coward, call me weak, I don't give a fuck. I had the rest of my life to deal with it.

Just not now.

For now, I was going to pretend.

I gave her a coy smile. "You'll see."

I was tempted to grab her hand and hold it as we walked down the streets; there were men leering at her from all directions and it was quite obvious I wasn't her boyfriend. I hated that. It happened all the time.

Instead I walked by her side, the chilly November breeze whistling in between us. I tried not to notice the way it turned her breasts into headlights. We couldn't get to the dark, anonymous club fast enough.

"What the hell is this?" she asked, eyeing the door to The Cecil. The strip club down-at-it's heels, nowhere near as classy as Brandi's Showgirls, but Brandi's cost a lot of dough and I wasn't about to spend that much on Perry, who looked like she was going to start running over the Granville Street Bridge any second and all the way home to Portland.

"It's our fun for the night," I told her, motioning her to go inside.

"I thought the hockey game was our fun for the night," she said and crossed her arms.

Oy, convincing her to partake in naked ladies might be harder than I thought.

I decided to turn on the charm. It was always tactic number one.

I leaned in closer to her. "Kiddo, the fun never ends when you're with me."

She narrowed her eyes into two rather seductive looking slits. "If you think I'm going into a strip club..."

"Oh, don't be such a pussy," I sniped. Tactic number two. Call her a pussy.

Her eyes widened for a second, then she brought an equally amusing sneer to her face. "I am not a...*pussy*. I just don't have any desire to see some tonight."

"But I do," I whined. "Please, Perry?"

Tactic number three. Beg.

"Seriously?"

I smacked her lightly on the arm. "You're no fun."

"I'm more fun than you can handle," she said and wagged her finger at me. Then she turned on her heel, flung open the door and marched into the club. She was extra hot when she was angry.

And there I was getting turned on again.

I sighed and followed her.

After the doorman collected our cover money (which I paid for - because I'm a gentleman), I led Perry straight toward the stage. I recognized the girl up there, wriggling her ass away. I didn't remember her name but I'd had a lap dance from her before. Not the best, not the worst.

I snuck a peek at Perry. She was putting on a brave face but I knew she was feeling as awkward as all fuck. You can always tell with her. Her shoulders hunch over a bit, like she's shielding herself from the world and though her mouth is set in a "don't mess with me" line, her eyes are sad, like she's about to be found out at any moment. She's vulnerable and she hates it.

I thought bringing her to the stage where the leerers and jeerers were would have been a good idea. Fun. I immediately knew it wasn't. I didn't like her like that. I liked her with her chin high and her chest out.

I put my hand on her shoulder, just for a moment, just for comfort, and pointed at an empty booth in a dark corner. I could only imagine how dirty it was (it's not like they sanitized the seats every hour) but I knew it was out of the way and hidden.

Once there, being careful not to wince at the sticky seat, I ordered us two Jack and Cokes and tried to put Perry at ease.

"Just pretend you're in Disneyland," I told her.

She managed to snort and look scared at the same time. "Yeah, a Disneyland where Ariel walks around topless."

"Hey, either way it smells like fish." I smiled.

She gave me a disgusted look. "You can be really gross sometimes."

I took that as a compliment. It meant I was getting under her skin.

We watched the dancer do her thing for a few moments, Perry trying to look and not look. Our drinks came and I told her, "Look at it this way. You pay cover going into any other bar nowadays. Might as well get a show to go with it."

I held up my drink to her. She did the same.

"Even though these drinks are probably ten dollars each?" she pointed out. I noticed her eyes moved away from mine. She probably didn't believe in that whole ten years of bad sex thing. Not that bad sex could ever happen if I was in her bed.

Jesus, Dex, I thought. *Get back on track.*

"Oh, it's worth it." Our glasses clinked. I watched her intently for any signs of loosening up. So far it wasn't going very well. She was looking all over the place, taking in everything in nervous little spurts. Her eyes eventually settled where everyone else's eyes were settled: the stage.

And why not? It was Marla up there. I didn't try and memorize the names of the strippers here but Marla was a gorgeous creature and gorgeous creatures deserved some of my respect. Unlike some of the snaggletoothed dancers who could barely waddle out a song, Marla had this old Hollywood vibe to her. She was still a bit of a whore, but at least one you could take out for dinner.

"Marla always has the best moves here, doesn't she," I found myself saying out loud, hypnotized by her movements. I'm sorry, but when there's a stripping naked woman nearby, you can't help but watch. Especially when it's Marla.

"You know her name?" Perry sounded incredulous. And a bit pissed off. If I had known any better I would have thought she was jealous. But the idea of that was ludicrous. It was probably her fuckload of insecurities coming into play again.

"You always remember the best ones," I explained. "That's not saying much."

I watched her squirm in her seat and wrestle with something in her head.

"Is this making you uncomfortable?" I asked her.

She gave me a brief but nasty look. "You'd like that, wouldn't you?"

She was kind of right. That was part of the plan.

I put a hurt look on my face. "You think less of me now."

The funny thing was, I almost wanted her to think less of me. I sometimes caught this starry-eyed gaze on her face, like she was looking at me with...I don't know, adoration. It was unwarranted. And dangerous. Yet, I still wanted to push her buttons, prod her over the edge. I wanted to challenge her, make her live beyond her bounds. And a major part of me wanted that adoration from her. But that was the part I let out only when I was jerking off. It was safer that way. Just a sore wrist to show for it.

I don't know if anything I was thinking had shown up on my face because Perry suddenly flushed even deeper. Then she laughed. "If anything, I think more of you."

I grinned.

"Good," I told her and tipped her cup so the drink was going faster into her mouth. Fuck. Talk about another turn on. She could hold a lot in her throat. "You're learning."

I held her eyes for a moment before we both looked away. We watched Marla grind until there was nothing left on her but pale skin and moody lights. We drank.

The waitress came by and I ordered two more doubles for us. She eyed Perry. I couldn't blame her. Perry had taken off her jersey because of the dirty sweat and heat in the room and her little black tank top did nothing but show off her breasts. I wasn't even sure how they were staying so high and perky. Young age, I guess. I had been trying not to stare at them for the last five minutes but now that the waitress was, I could too. And I couldn't have gotten harder if I tried. Thank god for the table.

The waitress gave me an appreciate look. "This your girlfriend? She's cute."

Perry was more than cute and no, she wasn't my girlfriend but I nodded anyway. I looked at Perry slyly. "She is cute, isn't she?"

Cute, pretty, so completely fuckable.

The ever present red of her cheeks deepened. Then the waitress leaned in closer and dear god, I could have shot a load right through the top of the table.

"Honey," she purred in Perry's ear. "With your eyes and those breasts, you should be up there too."

Then she left to get our drinks. Poor Perry, she looked like she wanted to climb under the table and die.

"Guess it doesn't matter what sex you are," she managed to get out, her eyes wide and innocent.

"Don't be so modest," I chided her. I looked at the stage where another stripper was grinding. Perry was better than any of these girls, better in so many ways, yet here she was feeling like she wasn't worthy. I didn't understand her problem at all. How could she have gone through life so far without noticing the looks she got from men?

The looks she got from *me*.

I watched her, taking in her unguarded features

"You've got a beautiful face," I found myself explaining to her. The Jack was quickly making its way through my system but I didn't care. I turned my focus to the stage and watched the stripper absently. "Gorgeous eyes. I mean I've rarely seen eyes like yours. Fuck, it's like looking out at the ocean and trying to read it as the weather's changing." OK, I wasn't making sense anymore. I continued anyway. "Perfect lips. The most adorable freckles and the tiniest little nose. You're like a sexy...bunny."

That settled it. I wasn't allowed to talk anymore. I couldn't believe I just called her a bunny rabbit. A sexy one at that. *Real smooth, Dex.*

I shot her a quick look. I would have thought she'd have some snappy one-liner to refute the bunny remark, but her mouth was slightly agape and she had nothing.

"Speechless? That's a start." I couldn't help but feel victorious.

The waitress chose that moment to hand us our drinks. After I paid her ($25!), Perry still hadn't said anything.

"Has no one ever complimented you before?" I asked, trying to get her to talk. I pushed her new drink into her hands, hoping she'd suck her current one back faster. I was feeling buzzed as shit and I needed her to get on board with me. The more sober and serious we got, the more I'd have to deal with that other bomb from earlier.

She shook her head. I still couldn't believe it. Were guys in Portland just fucking idiots or what the hell was going on here? Sure she wasn't model skinny like some people I knew, but she was all woman and what guy didn't want that? More to play with, in my opinion.

I sighed. She wasn't going to get it any time soon. I could sit here and tell her how gorgeous I thought she was but until she believed it, whatever I said was falling on deaf ears. And yes, I went on to tell her she was beautiful and had a devastating ass and whatever else I threw in to sweeten the pot, but really, why the hell should she care what I thought anyway?

I wasn't her boyfriend. I was just her partner.

Her partner with a raging, seam-splitting hard on.

And I couldn't take it anymore.

I shot her a quick look, trying to convey nonchalance. "I'll be right back."

Then I left her alone in the club.

There's no pride or shame in where I went. Yes, I went to the bathroom. Yes, I went there to jack off. No, most men don't actually jack off in the bathroom of a strip club. Believe it or not, it's not really a very sexual place. It's a place for frat boys and lonely old men, not a wankfest. It's rare for a stripper to get you so worked up that you have to escape for a few moments.

But Perry wasn't a stripper. Perry was Perry. And this was bound to happen, from the beginning. It was just better this way for me, to get it out of the way before I did something really stupid and started coming onto her or something. Or coming. In general. You know, in my pants.

It didn't take long at all and I came out of the bathroom feeling dirtier than ever. Fuck, just what was happening to me? This was the man I'd become?

In typical fashion I decided to revel in it. I motioned for Marla to come over. She was leaning against the bar, scouting the bar for eager participants. Upon seeing me, her face lit up.

"Hey Sugar," she said in her silky voice. She put her hand on my forearm and squeezed it. "Haven't seen you in a long time."

"Been busy," I told her, grinning cheekily. "I was wondering if you could give my partner over there a lap dance."

"The girl I saw you come in with?" she asked incredulously. "I thought she was your girlfriend."

"No, she's not." I didn't want to elaborate. "But she needs to let loose, I thought you could help her."

"Isn't that your job?"

"Not yet."

She smirked at me through sticky pink lips. "So this is all for her benefit, is it?"

I reached down and smacked her barely clothed ass. "Go on, I'll make it worth your while." I slipped out a few twenties from my pocket and stuffed them in her bra.

She flashed me her expensive veneers. "No problem."

She sashayed toward Perry. By some wonderful luck, the song "Stripsearch" by Faith No More came on. I decided to hang around by the bar, lurking in the background, watching, listening. What had Perry called me earlier? A pervy weirdo? Yeah, that sounded about right.

There was no doubt in anyone's mind that I was the biggest pervy weirdo around.

And considering where I was, that was saying a lot.

I watched Marla approach Perry, her fake breasts in Perry's face. They exchanged a few words and I could see how fish-out-of-water Perry was. But surprisingly, she hadn't turned Marla away. I expected to see Marla attempt to grind on her, then see Perry flip out like she often does. That would have been enough to fulfill my dirty mind. But instead, Perry sucked it up and let Marla do her thing.

My eyes were laser beams on them both as Marla slid up and down Perry's thigh. I watched as Marla's top came off and slithered down to the floor. I couldn't have been more turned on if I tried. Yet there was this strange feeling of pride amongst the perverseness. I was actually proud of Perry.

It was mesmerizing. Hands down, the best $40 I could have ever spent. It was a memory I'd draw on in the future when my life was down the shitter and I couldn't remember ever feeling free.

When Marla finally finished, she slipped on a robe that seemed to come from nowhere and worked her way past me. She shot me a sly look out of the corner of her eye and I leered at her form appreciatively. Credit was needed where credit was due. Then I took in a deep breath and got ready to face my partner who may or may not have been waiting to kill me.

I approached the table cautiously, putting my feelers out. Perry's face was flushed pink again but I didn't know if it was because she was angry or embarrassed. Or both.

I took the seat across from her. She now looked a bit enlightened, like she was having an epiphany of sorts. Dear god, I hoped she hadn't liked the lap dance *too* much.

"What?" I asked.

"Nothing," she said. *Lying.* What a liar. She got a lap dance from the hottest woman in the club (aside from her, of course), a dance that her partner orchestrated for his own perverse pleasure, and she had *nothing* to say? I'd be lying if I said I wasn't incredibly disappointed. Yeah, the dance was totally for me but I'd hoped she'd, I don't know, at least thank me for the experience.

She pulled out her phone and let out a puff of air as she looked at it. I first thought she had gotten another angry tweet or anonymous blog comment but she was just looking at the time. It was getting late. She obviously wanted to put it all behind her.

"You want to go?" I asked, knowing it was probably the smart thing to do.

She nodded with an unsure smile on her lips. "I had fun though. Obviously you had more fun than me, though you weren't in the bathroom all that long."

Could she have known what I was doing in there? I was probably a hell of a lot more obvious than I had thought. Did she think it was because of her though, and did she like it? That's what I wanted, needed, to know. I studied her face, trying to read the slight melancholy look in her eyes, the tense way her jaw was set, how soft and pouty her lips were when the smile wore off.

"I hope you remember what I've said," I told her quickly before polishing off the rest of my drink. I got out of the seat and held my hand out for her. I was still a gentleman, remember?

She let out a small laugh, one that lit up her whole face. God, she was gorgeous.

"Every time I think of strip clubs, I shall think of you," she said in such a feminine voice that the minute she put her hand in mind, I grasped it hard. I pulled her right up into me, feeling her breasts hot against my chest, her heart beating fast and steady.

My chin grazed the top of her head and I caught a whiff of her coconut shampoo. I closed my eyes for the briefest instance and in that instant we weren't in a dirty strip club in Vancouver. We were somewhere else where it was just her and I and nothing else mattered.

It took all my effort to take a step back and hold her at arm's length when all I wanted to do was lean over, grab her firmly around the waist, and taste the inside of her mouth.

I was just so tired of wanting something I absolutely knew I could never have.

NINE

DIGGING THE GRAVE

"Truth or dare?"

The minute Perry uttered those words, I knew I was totally screwed. Listen, people, I don't care who you're playing with and how close to them you are but truth or dare is never a good idea.

Ever.

You're demanding truth when life is better, smoother, with lies. And just in case you didn't feel like being honest, you had a dare. Dares are the stupidest shit ever because no one ever does them. They don't! You ask "truth or dare" and they say "dare!" and then you say, "I dare you to eat this entire jar of wasabi" and guess what? They don't do it! They never do it. Why, oh why, didn't I bring a jar of wasabi on this camping trip? If I had, I would have made Perry eat it instead of pouring her heart out to me.

OK, so that sounds kinda uncaring. Mean, maybe. And really it was the game "I Have Never" that started it all. Truth or dare shouldn't get all the blame.

But Perry is already my soft spot – my weak spot. It

didn't make me feel good to hear about how her douchebro boyfriend Mason had cheated on her. It made me feel wretched and terrible to learn that she had an abortion. And when I had to deny her dare...because it was the right thing to do? It broke my fucking heart.

"Truth or dare?" she had asked me.

Perhaps I brought it on myself. I didn't want to say truth because I knew what truth she was after and I didn't want to go there. Oblivious and ignorant, that was my way. Let's worry about the ghosts and lepers, but screw dealing with our real problems.

So I said, "Dare."

And she said...

"I dare you to kiss me."

As I said. Heartbreaking.

Perry was leaning on her elbows, eyes glazed but still beautiful, swaying back and forth from the throes of alcohol. She looked so earnest. So real. So...everything I wanted.

And I was going to have to say *no*.

It broke my fucking heart.

I tried to wipe the fear off my face. I smiled at her, though I don't know if it was convincing enough.

"I can't do that," I said desperately trying to hide the gravity in my voice. She couldn't know how it affected me. I had to treat it like a game.

She looked at me with pleading round eyes. Talk about a dagger to my heart.

"But you have to. You said during the hockey game...if you were dared. This is your dare."

Crapity crap crap. Of course I said that as a joke, and even if I wasn't joking I didn't think she'd hang on to it. I never thought she take that as word. I never really thought she'd *want* to take that as word. But that was all before Jenn's phone call.

That one phone call.

Everything was so different now. I knew the dare. And I knew the truth. And the truth was that if I did as she dared, I would lose myself to her completely. There were so many times already on the trip, when the ghosts spooked me out and I was afraid and my adrenaline was running higher than anything, that I wanted to turn to her. I wanted to shut her up with my lips, to take her in my arms.

But I couldn't.

There was Jenn. And even though sometimes I thought Jenn didn't matter, she did now. She mattered and so did my unborn child. I swallowed hard. This was the most I thought about it in days.

"It's kind of inappropriate," I explained weakly. I know how lame that sounded. I wanted to tell her that I wanted nothing more than to kiss her. But what fucking good could ever come of that?

She tried not to look rejected. She really did. But it was clear as all hell on her face. In the way she bit her lip. The way she stopped swaying. The sadness in her eyes.

"Whatever, you have to take truth then."

She smiled at me coyly. It was false. Oh so false. She was shutting down. Turning her soul away from me. She laid herself out there and I turned it down.

It fucking burned.

Well, if she was going to shut down, I was going to open up.

"Ok, give me the truth then," I encouraged.

She smiled. And I knew what was coming.

"What was the phone call about?"

See. I knew it. I knew that was the plan for this game all

along. But it didn't matter. I owed this to her. I could at least explain why I couldn't kiss her...and why she and I could never ever be.

I took in a deep breath.

"Jennifer is pregnant."

TEN

WHEN GOOD DOGS DO BAD THINGS

I WAS ALREADY AWAKE WHEN THE TERRIBLE WAILING sound came crashing through the trees. I couldn't sleep at all with Perry crammed up next to me in our sardine can sleeping bag, especially when my thoughts were torn between her and Jenn. It was all starting to sink in. I had never been so fucking screwed in my whole life. I couldn't even blame anyone for this except myself. Jenn was on the pill and we'd been having frequent sex for three years straight. The pill wasn't magic. Logic says that one of the little guys was bound to slip past the barrier. I suppose most guys, if they weren't freaking the fuck out, would be a bit proud at this accomplishment. You know, "my sperm is so powerful it punched that pill in the uterus" or something like that. But I felt scared shitless.

If I'm being honest here, there was a time when having a child wouldn't have been so scary. When I was with Abby, and in stupid, obsessive love, I often thought about us having a family together. A baby, marriage, the whole shebang. I wanted to give a little version of myself the life I never had. I wanted to live vicariously through them and pretend my whole fucked-up life never happened. That's a pretty selfish way of looking at having children, but come on, it's me we're dealing with here. If you looked up "selfish" in the dictionary, my picture would be there.

I guess I should have been happy then when Jenn told me that she was going to have the baby whether or not I was involved. That stung. And that was a weird feeling. Our relationship had always been an easy ride. We never expected much of each other. No one's heart or feelings were on the line. We had an understanding of companionship and sex. Did I love Jenn? No, I didn't. I never did. And it was for the best. It was for the best, for my best, that I never loved anyone.

But now that she was prepared to take this baby and do it on her own, without me, I felt rejected or something. Like I wasn't needed. I was just the sperm donor and she would take off with a little part of me that I secretly wanted...just under different circumstances. So, naturally I would tell Jenn I'd stick by her. And I'd even marry her if she wanted. But either way, I was going to be unhappy. Talk about making your bed and lying in it.

Thankfully the horrible wailing crashed into my thoughts like a jackhammer and stopped my late night downward spiral. Now I had something more pressing to fear.

Lepers.

The scream continued, coming closer and then moving away in spurts, curdling my blood with each wail. It sounded like a cat being raped by a sad monkey; pained, terrified and sad.

I was terrified and Perry was sleeping away, looking peaceful. Well, not if I could help it. I wasn't going to go through this all alone. If I had to suffer she had to too. And yes, if you look up "chickenshit" in the dictionary, my picture's there, too.

I put my hand on her shoulder and shook her awake.

She looked up at me with clouded eyes.

"What? What's going on?" she mumbled.

A gut-wrenching, piss-your-pants cry shot through the tent.

"What the hell is that?" she exclaimed, the fright filling her face where ignorant sleep had been just seconds before.

"I don't know, it just started. I think it's the nut."

She looked at me as if I was the nut. I explained to her about the nutty leper that once lived in the colony.

"Jesus," she swore.

Won't save you now, I thought. Actually, now that she was awake, I felt less scared. This was exactly the type of thing I should be filming!

"We have to get this on film!" I very ungracefully wiggled out of the sleeping bag and made a dash for the Super 8.

"What, no! You can't go out there," she cried out from behind me.

I grabbed my shoes. I couldn't miss this.

"Yes, I can, I have to."

"No!" she screamed. Her pitch matched the lepers. It made me put down my shoes and look at her. I hadn't heard her that scared the whole time on the island. She looked frightened as hell too. She was literally shaking in the sleeping bag, two seconds away from one of her panic attacks.

"You can't go out there!" she continued. "There are things out there that want to hurt you."

Say what?

"What things, what are you talking about?"

She gave me a pleading look. "Please, Dex, just trust me."

That wasn't a good enough answer for me.

I shook my head. "No way, I'm not missing this. You stay here."

I unzipped the tent, a fresh blast of night air whipping through, when she reached over and grabbed me by the arm, her nails digging into my skin.

"Don't leave me!" she pleaded, her voice strained with fear and agony.

I relented, letting her hands pull me away from the flap. She looked like she was on the verge of tears. I didn't think I could leave her in this state.

"I need you," she whispered.

That was a new one. It stirred up something strange and foreign in my chest. No one ever needed Dex Foray.

"You need me?" I asked, my throat feeling thick.

She pulled me closer, her grip growing tighter. Something was happening. Something that made me forget all about that nut in the forest. I barely heard the cries anymore. I was too caught up in Perry's eyes, the way they shone in the darkness. Whatever this something was, it was crackling with heat, drawing us to each other like a tightened rope, burning around each other.

"I need you," she said with such determination that it was like declaring war.

I watched her lips as she said it.

If she wanted war, she was going to get war.

I smiled.

Then I threw caution to the wind and did the thing I'd been dreaming about doing.

I lunged for her, grabbing her face in my hands, bringing her mouth to mine. It felt better than I thought it would, feeling her, tasting her, my tongue going after hers like I was trying to tame it. If I kept this up I would fucking eat her alive.

I pushed her back onto the sleeping bag and tried to devour her as much as I could. None of this could wait, there was urgency involved, the explosion of too many feelings and missed opportunities. This was what I always wanted, what I fucking jacked off to every damn night. And now she was beneath me, her soft hands touching me around the waist, trying to bring me into her, as if she couldn't get enough too. She pulled my shirt off, scratched her nails on my chest like a cat in heat. I retaliated by sucking on her neck, tasting the sweat and whatever else she was made of. I pushed the envelope, not caring if we were going too far, and began to take off her pants. Fuck these fucking clothes, I wanted skin on skin.

I put my hand under her shirt, feeling the goosebumps of her skin at my contact. Her nipples were sword-sharp and begging to be squeezed along with the rest of her breast. She felt like a dream, a cloud. But it wasn't enough.

She wanted more too. She reached down and pulled her top over her head and I saw Perry's succulent chest in all its glory. I wished it wasn't so dark, so I could see more than just the hint of creamy skin on a hot, rounded silhouette. Her eyes were heavy with lust, begging for me to continue. Oh god, I was trying so fucking hard not to come and I didn't even have my pants off.

I went for her neck and chest again, licking every inch of her, consuming every good thing she was. She moaned and I almost couldn't handle it.

Then her hands were at my pants. I was more than happy to get them off but when her firm grip found my cock, felt how stone hard I was, I knew I was in big trouble.

I groaned with pleasure. Loudly. I wanted more but an extra second of groping and it would all be over very fast. And I still had plans. Very wet plans.

I moved back and out of her reach.

I was in control now.

I parted her soft, full legs with my hands and brought my head south. I had a few moves to give her before the main course.

I took my finger and flicked the yielding skin underneath her knee. Then I twisted my head around and did the same act with my tongue, flicking it gently in teasing motions. Her leg tensed up and she made a whimpering sound. She was relishing it like I hoped she would. Her legs even parted more, an obvious invitation.

I accepted.

I took my hand and spread her lips open, running a finger up and down her clit. She was swollen as fuck and as wet as a Slip N' Slide, and it was only going to get more slippery.

I put my lips to her thick wet ones and pushed in my tongue. She was perfect. She tasted perfect, her own type of musky perfume that made my cock even harder until it was flat up against my stomach. It cried out for her touch, begged to come but I couldn't indulge it. This was about her.

She needed me and I was going to give her what she needed.

Her hips were rising, trying to meet my face. My tongue was pushing her over the edge. I didn't want her to go over yet. I wanted to see her, all of her, when she did.

I pulled back and brought my chest onto hers, our sweat mingling. I put two fingers inside of her where they disappeared into the wetness, like she was hungry. With my other hand I grabbed hold of her soft hair and made a fist in it. I pulled it back slightly and her eyes flew open at the delicious pain. I tugged and stroked, hands and fingers, hair and slickness. I did it over and over again until I was almost coming myself. It was painful for me, to hold it back, but I had to.

When she finally came, it was the most beautiful, amazing, fucktastic, heart-grabbing moment of my life. She cried out, an act of instinct. I could hear the pleasure rolling out of her mouth in waves before it slowed to a whimper. It almost sounded hurt but I knew better.

I brought my fingers out of her and rested them on her stomach. I was tempted to lick them off but that probably would have skeeved her out and I didn't want to do anything to ruin the moment.

When she came back down from her high, she rolled her head over and stared at me. I stared right back. We had just crossed a major barricade. I was as turned on as fucking hell and we needed to leave things as they were. I gave her what she needed and that's all I needed.

She reached for my face with her hand and tenderly stroked the side of my cheek. Her look said everything and it was too much. Reality began to sink in, competing with my dick for bragging rights.

What the fuck just happened? What the hell had I done to *us*?

Perry might have picked up on the change, I don't know, but she started reaching for my cock and I wasn't having any of that. Believe me, I wanted nothing more than to ram it in her, to really feel how wet she was, to know her from the inside and embrace me like no one else could. I was hard as iron and it was going to go to waste without being inside her.

"I'm sorry," I said feebly. "I can't."

"You can't what?" she asked. She didn't know. She didn't know how things would go if I continued. How further down the hole she and I would fall. We didn't even have a fucking condom, did she really want to end up pregnant? Perhaps with another abortion? Did I want to end up with another version of Jenn?

No. That wasn't fair. If Perry got pregnant that would be something entirely different. But that wasn't our reality. I wasn't with her. I was just her partner. I was with Jenn and that's who I deserved to spend the rest of my life with.

I just got Perry off, gave into the tension that seemed to wrap around us every time we were together. It was a mistake, even if it was the most unregrettable mistake I ever made.

"I don't want to hurt you," I told her. "And I will."

And I knew from the look in her big eyes, I already did.

If you look up "Biggest Douchebag on the Planet" in the dictionary, you'll see my picture.

ELEVEN
SHE LOVES ME NOT

SOMETIMES YOU CAN FORESEE CERTAIN MOMENTS IN your life. For me, it's usually a moment based on a lie. Cause and effect. You lie, you hide something from the world and you know one day someone will uncover the truth. And you know when that happens, it won't be pretty.

It will be ugly.

It will be the screaming face of your partner and she howls at you. The tears in her eyes that she's trying so hard to hold back. It's that look in her face that you just stabbed her in the gut and kicked over the side of a cliff. It's all the trust she ever had in you coming leaking out like an invisible stream of lost promises.

This was Perry the moment she found out that it had been Jenn all this time leaving the anonymous comments. I didn't imagine it going down any other way. I knew I'd be driving that sword into her. I knew she'd break inside. Suffer.

Or maybe it's that I'd be the one breaking. I'd suffer, from knowing what a dipshit I was. Perry and me, it was always one step forward, two steps back. I'd felt like we were finally making ground and then I had to tell her the truth.

The truth always sets my ass back.

She had turned away from me, whimpering her words through anger. "Why the hell didn't you tell me?"

What a place for it all to come out too. Locked in the dark basement of a haunted mental asylum. Actually, it was quite fitting. We had been driving each other insane for too long.

I reached out for her in the darkness, my hand resting on her shoulder.

She whipped around like a caged animal. A glimpse of feral hate in her eyes.

"Don't you fucking touch me!" she screamed, her voice echoing in the damp room.

No. I couldn't listen to that. I couldn't bear to have this between us. I needed to touch her, to know there was some part of her still mine.

Instinctively I grabbed her wrists and held on tight.

"I'm sorry," I said, searching her eyes for something. Anything.

"Let go of me!" she roared. I had found something. She was about to punch me in the face. I knew that look all too well.

Fuck, I was a jackass.

"Fine, punch me!" I yelled back at her, frustration rising. "But you have to listen to me first."

She wouldn't have any of it. "You're a fucking liar!"

And I was. I gripped her wrists tighter and pulled her up to me, needing her to listen, to see me, to hear me out. She relented, her dark hair whipped around her face in a frenzy. But she let me hold her up to me. She let me speak.

"Put yourself in my shoes Perry, please," I begged.

"She's my girlfriend, you're my partner. What was I supposed to do? Who was I supposed to protect?"

She closed her eyes, shutting me out. It felt like she was giving up. I didn't want the fire to die in her, I just wanted her to give me a chance to explain.

I sighed and let go of her hands. I didn't even know if explaining would help.

She slowly walked away without giving me a glance. Perry was defeated, and after all the strength I'd seen in her lately, it pained me to know it was me who did it to her.

"Baby," I called out to her, my voice trailing in the cold air.

"Don't you fucking call me that!" she exploded. "You don't get to. Especially after what you just said."

She was hurt. More hurt and angry than I had thought.

Why? What else was there?

I took a few cautious steps toward her. "Why is this bothering you?"

She let out an evil laugh. I couldn't see her face but I knew there was no humor in it. "Heaven forbid this should bother me."

"Did you want me to tell you?" I asked carefully.

"What the hell do you think?"

"Did you think I owed it to you?" And there I was again, digging, poking, looking for something to satisfy me. God, I knew what I wanted to hear.

Did she?

"I guess," she admitted. "I would have told *you*."

"Why?" I coaxed. I took another step toward her.

She slowly turned her head to look at me, maybe to warn me not to come any closer.

"Because..." her voice trailed off. I saw the outline of her throat as she swallowed hard. "You're..."

What? I'm what?

"Perry," I said, my voice shaking a bit.

She was now looking at the ground. In the shadows I could see her brow contracting. She was having an inner argument with herself. I didn't know if the side I wanted to win would win.

"What?" Fear rippled from her in waves.

She knew what I was going to ask. And I had to ask it anyway.

After all these months together, sleeping in the same bed, the night in the tent, the way my thoughts revolved around her very essence twenty-four hours a day. After almost dying, always saving each other, always pushing and pulling and hurting each other. I had to know how she really felt.

If she answered yes, I'd give in. And I'd tell her everything I was hiding. Everything I fought against every day. I would tell her the truth.

No more lies.

"Are you in love with me?"

And there. It was out there. I was admitting nothing myself but it had to be obvious that I was asking for a reason. That I wanted her to say yes. I needed her to say she loved me.

Then I would be a bit safer when I fell.

Her eyes went wide at the question. I guess it caught her off guard. Or she was a good actress. She'd certainly improved on camera.

"Excuse me?" she squeaked.

I took a few more steps toward her, filling her with my shadow.

"Do you love me?"

Please say yes.

Oh fuck, say yes Perry.

There was nothing but silence. That was bullshit. I had to know.

"Perry," I said again, more urgent. "Do you love me?"

She breathed in deep, a short sharp sound. She steadied herself and looked me in the eye. I looked back. There was no softness there. It was only hard edged and glinting, like a sword. That stabbing blade.

"No," she said simply. "I don't."

I was wrong. I had it all turned around.

I didn't put the sword into her. I only gave her the sword.

She's the one who just put it in me.

TWELVE
MAXWELL'S SILVER HAMMER

Sometimes things end out of the blue; one minute it's going, next minute...it's gone. Sometimes they crumble slowly, like your favorite pair of boxer briefs. You wear them every day cuz they cup your balls just so and don't ride up the legs and sooner or later they become a second skin. You even avoid washing them too often, as rank as that is, because you fear the washing machine will agitate things, shake them up, pull apart those fibers. But eventually, it's going to end. Your underwear will disintegrate. One tug in a fit of mindless passion or just pulling them down to use the can, and SNAP. There's nothing left to hold it together. You're naked. And your ass is cold.

I knew things were over, really over, when I was about to pull my own underwear off. And couldn't.

Jenn had gotten out of the shower and was done slathering her naked body with that Victoria's Secret arsenic-scented lotion. She was flashing me the come-hither eyes, the ones that usually created a o-to-6o boner in five seconds. But though the lil dude got a bit hard – it does that when I see naked women, I can't help it – it never got past the chubby stage.

And that's when I knew this was it. This was the end. If we didn't have sex, what did we have? Nothing. Absolutely butt-fuck nothing. Just a pair of miserable people hanging onto each other for the sake of...I don't know? Not companionship. Not love. Maybe Fear. Boredom.

Loathing.

"What's wrong?" she purred. She didn't understand why my hands weren't pulling down my drawers, why I wasn't stroking myself in anticipation.

What was wrong? *Are you really that clueless?* I thought. It was all hitting me now like a ton of bricks. How about Perry, Rebecca and Emily being just outside the door? How about finding out you've been fucking screwing around behind my back for who the hell knows how long? And with Bradley? Sir Swagger Douchington the Fuck?

I didn't say these things though. I didn't want her to know that I knew. I just knew it was done for. And whatever chance I had for happiness, happiness that I didn't really deserve, it wasn't in our bedroom. It wasn't with a Wine Babe in all her gorgeous, black-souled glory. It was out in the kitchen. Where a brave, dark-haired beauty was giggling with her new friends.

"I'm not in the mood," I said brusquely as she started reaching for my waistband. I had forgotten that she liked it when I said no. Not that I ever really said no.

She wiggled her perfect bum in the air. Anyone else would have said I was gay for not being turned on by Jenn there on all fours, golden naked honey on white sheets. But making out with a guy seemed like a mighty fine alternative to getting sucked into a vortex of lies and fake nails.

"Dex," she said, her voice getting pitchy.

"I need to get ready. So do you, it's a big night and we're running out of time," I told her and stepped far out of her reach. To cement my point I quickly slipped on my black dress pants. They were itchy as hell and rarely worn but I wanted to look good tonight. I had someone else I needed to impress. I hoped they would do my ass justice.

I ignored Jenn, turning my back to her and searching for matching socks. I was sort of mindlessly looking, purposely busying myself until she dropped it and lost interest. It didn't take too long. Jenn knew she had to get ready too and I'd bet my dog's farts that she was trying to impress Perry as well.

I heard her sigh and get off the bed. She slipped some ugly '80s Kim Cattrall type dress over her head, pottered about finding her heels, then finally left the room.

As soon as the door clicked shut, I breathed out a sigh of relief. Believe it or not, I felt a bit bad. Jenn's self-esteem was surprisingly fragile and I didn't like going out to a party with both of us off-kilter. But then again, she brought this on herself. So had I.

Maybe you belong together after all, I thought. Who was I to judge her when I was just as much of an ass?

A giggle resounded from outside the door and shook the pity party out of my pants. Perry. She was all I needed to think about tonight. Not Jenn. Not even myself. Just Perry. I needed to do right by her and no one else. Maybe then that nasty voice in my head would shut the fuck up.

I slipped on a white dress shirt and black jacket and stared myself down in the mirror. Maybe it was because I wasn't especially tall, but I always felt like a monkey in a suit. But it looked OK. I knew I looked handsome, maybe even dashing in that wannabe Bond way. I also looked strangely alert for someone who nearly died the night before.

I stopped looking at myself before I turned into one of those guys who give pep talks to their reflection ("Yeah, work that mustache, you stud, chicks fucking dig the creeper look") picked up my tie and made my way out into the apartment where Beastie Boys was blaring.

Jenn was leaning against the counter with a glass of wine in hand. She raised her brows invitingly, which meant she wasn't all that mad about earlier. Perhaps she was already drunk.

"Tie or no tie?" I asked as I walked toward her.

Then, like I was pulled into some cosmic pulse, I paused and looked over at the stereo.

It was a vision of teal satin. And breasts. Oh my god, the breasts.

My eyes locked onto Perry and my breath was stolen. It wasn't just the breasts though – or the nip and curve of her waist and hips, a rolling highway that made me break erection speed records. She looked truly beautiful, comfortable. She was fresh, alive, glowing and...just so fucking real.

I don't know how long I was staring at her from across the room, my eyes taking a dip in her own blue pools, but it was enough that my dick was straining hard against my fly and Jenn said something about taking a picture to make it last longer.

I didn't need to. That moment would always be burned in my head. That moment when I knew that I was way in over my head. I was fucked.

THIRTEEN
MR. SELF DESTRUCT

WHEN WE ENTERED THE APARTMENT, THE TENSION followed us in. There wasn't even any Fat Rabbit to break the newly formed ice between us; he was locked in the bathroom. It was a peculiar kind of ice too. It held us tightly wound, unable to let our guard down. It was a wall that came up as soon as we broke apart in that snowy alley. Fuck, I wanted that again, that feeling of her legs wrapped around me. I needed us to thaw.

Perry walked across the kitchen and leaned against the island counter, her back to me. She kicked off her shoes, the berry heels dangling seductively off her foot. Her head was down, her upper back arched up, leaving the expanse of her shoulders and creamy smooth skin ripe and open for the taking. I kicked off my own shoes and took off my jacket in anticipation.

We needed to thaw. Ice melts with heat and I was packing enough heat in my pants that it pained me. Something needed to be done, for both of us.

I walked toward her carefully, feeling like I might scare her off and ruin the opportunity if I made any sudden movements. Keeping with that theme, I cautiously pushed some of her hair off of her shoulders, all to make room for my lips.

She didn't flinch from my touch. She had expected it.

She wanted it and I wanted her.

I wanted nothing but her, now and forever.

I placed my lips where the wasp had stung her. It was sign of what she was willing to risk for me and I owed her so much more than just my kiss.

I kissed along her back, down her shoulder, feeling her shake beneath me. I tried to get her to face me, but she wasn't thawed yet. I pressed my chest against her, pressed everything against her, and kissed at the corner of her mouth. I needed her to turn to me, give herself, all of her.

She did. She barely made it around before I was all over her, my hands searching her face, her hair, trying to take her all in at once.

There was no turning back tonight.

I put my hands at her small waist and lifted her onto the counter. She wrapped her legs around me again and I responded by hiking up her satiny dress until it was above her hips.

Oh, holy fuck.

I almost drooled on her as I stared at her open on display. My hunger was already insatiable before this.

As was hers. Her eyes looked ravenous, uncontrollable. She reached forward and ripped open my shirt. The buttons flew off. It would have been funny if my head wasn't so clouded with lust. I unzipped her dress and pulled it down until her full breasts spilled out like heavy, round dreams from heaven. I tried drowning in them, tasting, licking like I couldn't get enough.

She leaned back and I realized she wanted more. I pushed her gently with my hand until her back was against the counter. Then I grabbed both her thighs and took a dive. I started by swirling my tongue up the soft inner part before I had enough teasing and got to the heart of it. Just like that time on D'Arcy Island, I was rewarded with hot, perfumed wetness. I ate her until she grabbed my head and pulled it up.

Had I done something wrong? I don't know what I'd do if this wouldn't go farther. Jack off for eternity, probably.

"Do you want me to stop?" I asked. Had I been too soft? Too rough. Fuck what the hell was it!?

"No," she said in a voice that made my hairs stand straight. "I want you inside me."

My eyes widened.

Done.

"Yes ma'am," I told her.

In seconds we were both naked as fuck, a first for us at the same time. She let her eyes rest on my cock and I was more than happy to say she looked scared. I couldn't blame her. I felt like I had been having blue balls for thirty-two years and I had a large rod of steel to show for it.

She wrapped her legs around me and brought me into her. I brought my fingers down and rubbed at her until I knew she was slick enough to handle me then I gripped my cock and put it inside. She was tight. So tight. I could barely handle it and my brain started going over the weirdest things to keep everything under control. I wasn't going to go this far and blow my load in two seconds. I wasn't in high school.

I let out a few short bursts of breath, trying to take it as slow as possible. She had other ideas. She put her nails into my ass and encouraged me to speed up. I tried to keep pace without losing everything. I let my hands and face roam all over her upper body, holding on to every moment, watching her every chance I could. Who knew when I'd get this chance again?

And then it came to the point where I couldn't take any of it anymore. Having sex with Perry was...well, I was surprised I lasted so long, especially when she'd smack me on the ass lightly and then grind me into her. But I wasn't about to come first. Somewhere I remembered my manners.

I started rubbing her again, feeling how warm she was. I went for broke. I thrust into her deeper and deeper, faster and faster until we both lost it. A mess of groans.

I came into her like a high-pressured hose. There was a moment where I saw her eyes and she saw me and suddenly we were somewhere else, another world of shimmering air. It seemed to last for all eternity.

And in that eternity I got a glimpse of myself.

That wasn't just fucking. That wasn't just long overdue. This was love.

I was head over heels in love with her. No, that didn't describe it. I was tear my fucking heart out and throw it at her, beg her to take it into hers. I was falling from the greatest heights with no safety net below. I was giving everything of my own life for hers, giving up every inch of my soul so she could wear it proudly. I was a former king on my knees in front of the queen. A jester begging for a chance. I was powerless, helpless and at her mercy.

And that was the one place I swore I'd never be again.

To love was to hurt.

I wasn't strong enough to survive it again if everything went wrong.

Against all my instincts, I pulled out of her and walked toward the bathroom without even a backward glance. It was all too much. Way too fucking much.

I lost everything before it even began.

I was reduced to a coward, hiding from future pain. How could I love someone who didn't love me? Even I didn't love me.

Eventually I came out of the bathroom and saw the door to the den closed. She was in there and lord knows what she was feeling or thinking. I felt so terrible having to hurt her the way I was going to. But I had no other choice. It was better this way, now. It would be superficial to her.

I slipped on my pajama pants and went to the couch. I was dazed, empty. Whatever ice had thawed was freezing over again, starting somewhere in my heart.

There, I thought. *This is safer. Better.*

I put my head in my hands and wondered what I'd say next.

Then she came out of the den. I heard her walk up to me. I didn't need to look at her to read the worry she was giving off.

"Are you OK?" she asked, her voice wavering.

Fuck me. And she was being polite about it. She cared. She really did.

But she doesn't love you, I told myself, almost yelling in my head. *She told you she doesn't love you and you saw the truth in her eyes. To love her means to hurt yourself.*

I could take pain but not that road again.

She put her hand on me. I jumped.

"Dex," she said, "Talk to me."

Right. Like talking would do any good. I tried talking to her before this whole mess started. I know what she said.

When I didn't answer her, she grabbed my arm and tried to pull it away from my head.

"Dex, please!" she yelled.

I looked at her. I had no idea what she saw.

Neither did she.

She leaned forward. "What is it? What happened?"

"Nothing happened," the words just fell out of me. "And I hope you remember it that way."

She sucked in her breath. "What do you mean by that?"

Oh, she knew.

I yanked myself out of her grip. "What do you think I mean?"

She wasn't biting. She looked defiant. Stubborn. Naïve.

"Dex, just tell me what you're talking about, you owe me this much."

I had to laugh. She didn't get it.

"I don't owe you anything, Perry."

It probably came out a little meaner than I expected. But this wasn't about me owing her. She had the chance to owe me and she turned her back.

"Dex, what the hell is wrong with you? Why are you acting like this?"

"Why are you acting like this," I shot back, annoyed. "All in my face and bugging me every fucking second."

OK. Now I was just being nasty. I couldn't help it. Whatever good there was in me was being replaced by anger. Anger was so much better than fear. To be the one inflicting pain was better than being in pain yourself.

"Bugging you?" she repeated. "We just had sex and you're freaking out like-"

"I'm not freaking out about it!" I snapped.

She was unfazed at my obviousness. "Then what the hell is this? Because we were all fine an hour ago before this happened."

I put my head back in my hands. She was right. We had been fine. We had been us. We had been perfect. Now the tables were turned and I didn't know which way was up.

"I knew this was a mistake. This changed everything."

I thought I heard a gasp from her. I didn't care anymore.

"This wasn't a mistake," she cried out. "How could you say that?"

I decided to drive the point home, enjoying my nastiness.

"Typical. You're reading too much into this."

Let's see if she had any real feelings over that.

She looked like I had punched her in the face. She leaned against the couch, gasping for breath and kind of crumpled over on herself. She looked like she was dying and I was the cause.

I didn't drive that point home, I speared her with it. My words were ripping her apart from the inside. But why? It was just sex to her, wasn't it? She didn't love me. Did she? Why was she hurting like this? It was just me. Just Dex.

"Perry," I asked cautiously. She stayed in her huddled position, like the life was being sucked out of her.

Her head snapped up and someone had replaced her eyes with that of a viper.

"What was this to you, Dex?" she sneered with bottomless hate. "A rebound? An itch you had to get out of your system? Another notch to add to your bedpost? Another person to screw around with, mentally and physically?"

Oh fuck. I couldn't speak.

She continued, her eyes fixing on mine bitterly, "OK then, guess it was all of the above. Glad I finally know how you feel."

Me feel?

Before I could process that she took off for the den. She was throwing all her clothes in her bag.

Packing.

I leaped to my feet and came for her. "Where are you going?"

I grabbed her arm but she got free and shoved me back, hard. I was shocked at her strength, at her anger that was bleeding out of her. I never expected this.

"You made your point Dex," she said as if she were spitting out old gum. "You've now been very clear."

"Perry, wait," I protested weakly, "you can't leave now, it's snowing, you're in your pajamas." I had no idea how I was going to explain but I had to do something. The last thing I thought she'd do was actually leave me. I thought we'd fight then talk about it. Like we always did.

"I'm leaving and I'm not coming back! Rebecca was right about you, you're nothing but a scared little boy!"

Rebecca had said that? No matter, I had to stop her. She was acting crazy. It wasn't supposed to go this way. She didn't care enough. She wasn't supposed to!

I grabbed her in a panic, anything to keep her. I brought her up to me, my grip tight, trying to understand, to hold on.

"Why do you care so much?!" I yelled at her. My voice cracked over the next bit, "You told me you didn't love me!"

With a huge gust of strength, she wrestled out of my grasp and stumbled to the door. I reached for her but she turned to me in fury. She looked me right in the eye and I saw the truth. I saw it all. And it was all too late.

"You're not the only who knows how to lie, Dex!"

And there it was.

The truth.

She loved me. She had lied. She loved me all this time.

She loved me, *me*.

And I ruined it.

She left into the icy night, her anchor bracelet ripped on the floor. She was gone out of my life, out of the show. I had everything I wanted in my hands, in my actual hands, and I destroyed it before it could even become anything. I crushed everything we already had. I drove the only relationship that meant anything to me into the ground and then buried it with six feet of dirt.

I collapsed to my knees, unable to come to terms with what I had done. At the precious thing I'd lost. It was more than missing a part of me. It was feeling like there was nothing left of me to exist in her absence.

When my knees didn't feel low enough, I fell to my side and curled up on the floor.

When the floor still wasn't low enough, I began to cry.

I remained that way, a mess of tears in the hallway, my hand clutching the remains of the bracelet, until Jenn returned from her night out. Even she took pity on me.

Anyone would have. What else can you feel toward a man who once held the world in his hands only to throw it all away?

You think, "How can he live with himself?"

Good question.

I'll let you know.

FOURTEEN
DEMON CLEANER

"DEX, OVER HERE!"

I scanned the restaurant looking for the source of the smooth English accent that called my name. I swear, Rebecca's voice was on par with Morgan Freeman's in the 'voices I'd like to narrate my life' category.

I saw her in the corner of the room and made my way to her. The restaurant was a hipster-ish pizza joint not too far from my apartment and at six p.m. it was absolutely bustling. She looked delicious as usual, dressed from head to toe in a form-fitting black dress that gripped her hips and set off her vampire-pale skin. Any man would give his left nut to have a night with Rebecca. Unfortunately for everyone she enthusiastically played for the other team.

She got out of her chair and went for a hug, her smile wider than normal. It had been a few weeks since I'd seen her last and it seemed we both were in a darker place then.

She wrapped her arms around me for a few tight seconds, then she stepped out of the embrace and placed her soft fingers around my bicep and gave another, heartier squeeze.

"So you've been sticking to it," she remarked, looking proud. "Good for you. You look fantastic."

I felt fantastic. OK, that was bullshit. But I felt better than I had in weeks.

"You look gorgeous," I told her honestly and sat down at our cozy booth.

She gave me a coy wave, simultaneously brushing off the compliment and reveling in it as only she knew how, and ordered herself a drink when the waiter came by. I ordered a Jack and Coke, naturally.

She waited for the waiter to leave before she looked at me, surprised. "Really?"

I leaned back against the soft leather seat. "What?"

"I thought you were turning over a new leaf."

I snorted. "I have. I'm going to the gym every day, running, I quit smoking, I quit my meds. I can't give up all my vices. I'm not a superhero."

She twisted her cherry red lips around. I could tell she was thinking back to Xmas, when she and Em came over to take me out for a holiday gathering at a pub. Thank fuck they had Jenn's old key to the apartment otherwise shit could have really gotten ugly. They found me faced down on the balcony in my underwear, unconscious, a half-empty bottle of bourbon beside me.

"That's...all done with," I said, feeling defensive. "You know I was in a bad place at that time."

She smiled sadly and gave me a slow nod. "I know. I'm not judging. Frankly, I don't think I could hang out with you if you weren't the vice type of guy."

"Well then you'll be pleased to know that I'm still drinking and I'm still wanking to porn."

"That's my boy," she said appraisingly. The waiter came back with our drinks and we cheersed over it.

"To friends," she said.

"To friends," I agreed.

I took a big slog of my drink, the bubbles fizzing my nose, causing me to tense up. With watering eyes I looked at Rebecca. She was staring at my arms with an odd look on her face.

"What?" I asked.

She shrugged. "I don't know Dex, your arms, your shoulders...you look really good. It's nice to see."

"Good enough to make you switch sides?" I joked knowing she was a lesbian until the day she died.

She took a sly sip of her drink. I had missed the harmless flirting with her.

"Well you better not tell Em then," I continued. "Actually, maybe you should tell her. See if she wants to get in on the Dex action too." I winked at her.

She giggled. "Oh you. Once a pig, always a pig. At least that hasn't changed."

I gave her a forced smile even though what she said stabbed at me a bit. Was that what she really thought of me? Is that what everyone thought of me now?

Her face fell, which meant I wasn't doing a very good job of keeping my emotions under wraps. It was harder now when I was off the medication. I felt everything ten-fold and it was impossible to ignore at times. I felt sorry for women for having to deal with this emotional shit most of their lives.

I cleared my throat and anxiously picked up the menu, absently looking for something to eat. Going off the meds also made me hungry – too hungry – another reason why working out was so important now.

"So how is Jenn?" I asked innocently.

Rebecca looked a bit shocked. She lowered her voice

and leaned in slightly. "Do you want me to tell you or do you want the truth?"

I shot her a quick glance, trying to play it cool. "It doesn't matter, I don't really care."

"She's doing well then. I'm not too happy about it but it makes working with her easier."

I sucked in my breath and nodded. "Oh yeah?"

Fuck Jenn. Why did I even ask that? Wait, I didn't care.

"Yeah," she continued, watching me carefully for some sort of meltdown. "I guess Bradley makes her happy. It's a weird sight to see. She's still an annoying cunt though."

I humored her choice of words with a smile and went back to trying to pick a pizza. I *was* grateful that Jenn was out of my life but it still hurt to hear what Rebecca was saying. I didn't miss Jenn, but I didn't think it was fair that she was happy and I was absolutely miserable most hours of the day. The only time I was vaguely OK was when I was running, lifting weights or jerking off.

Rebecca reached over and placed her hand on mine, trying to get my eyes to meet hers. "You did the right thing Dex."

"Right," I mumbled.

"Just because..." she trailed off.

I gave her a sharp look. I didn't want her to finish that sentence.

She didn't. She just tapped my hand. "You know you did the right thing. You and Jenn breaking up was long over-due. You deserve someone better than that."

I didn't. But I appreciated the lie.

I smiled quickly and went back to the menu. I was distracting my head with the different toppings I could order when my phone rang.

I shot her an apologetic look and wondered if it was

Jimmy. He had been hounding me lately about coming back to Experiment in Terror. After Perry quit and after I had my little downward spiral full of shame and loathing and Cheetos and bourbon, the show was the last thing on my mind. When Perry left, I left too. Now that I was pulling myself out of the greasy orange-stained hole, Jimmy wanted my services again. Talk about a company that sucks you back in. But without Perry, I didn't see a whole lot of point to going forward. Without her, I wanted to do something, anything else.

I fished the phone out of my pocket and quickly glance at the screen. It wasn't Jimmy at all. It was some other number.

My heart stopped beating. I looked at Rebecca.

"Where is area code 503?" I asked quickly.

"Huh?"

"Area code 503!" I repeated in a panic.

Her face grew paler. "Portland."

I couldn't move. I couldn't breathe. Luckily Rebecca snatched the phone out of my hand and answered it for me before the caller hung up.

"Hello?" she asked. She frowned, listening. "Yes he is. May I ask who is calling?"

I bit my lip, my chest was growing tight with lack of oxygen. She looked at me, her eyes wide, her mouth dropping a little bit.

"Hi Ada, it's Rebecca," she said. "What's going on, are you OK?"

I immediately put my hand out for the phone. I still wasn't breathing but I was functioning.

She eyed me and nodded. "OK, calm down, I'm just going to give you to Dex here."

She placed the phone in mine and twitched her head in

the direction of the doors. It seemed like it was something I'd need to take in private.

I gave her a quick smile and put the phone to my ear as I got out of the booth.

"Ada?" I asked, making my way past the crowded tables.

"Dex?" I heard her young, tiny voice from the other end.

"Hi, what's up? Is Perry OK?" I didn't want to ask it, I felt like I had no right to, but I couldn't see any other reason for Ada to call. It had been too long since we had our falling out, the time to be reprimanded had past. And somewhere in my black heart, the minute I asked it, I knew that Perry *wasn't* OK.

I was lucky to have made it out of the restaurant and onto the chilled street when Ada said, "No, she's not OK. Something's happened to her."

I almost dropped the phone. Something had to give, so I did. I leaned against a brick wall and let my legs give out, and slid down until I was sitting on the ground.

"Dex?" she cried out. "Are you there?"

I closed my eyes and swallowed the fear. "Yes. I'm here. What happened?"

"I don't know."

"Is she hurt?" My voice cracked. I swallowed hard, shooting out little prayers in between the answers.

"Not really."

"Ada..."

"I don't know Dex. I shouldn't even be calling you. I just don't know what to do. I think she's possessed. She's...she's not herself, I've seen things too, things that are after her. They have her strapped to her bed now."

"Who are they?"

"My parents. Maximus."

"Maximus?!" I roared. People on the street looked at me and quickened their pace as they went past. I didn't care. The rage was almost undeniable. "What the fuck is he doing there?"

"He and Perry are, well I don't know. He's a douchecanoe, that's all that matters. Dex, she's gone. She's going. I don't know what to do. We did a house cleanse and then Maximus turned his back on us and is making it look like Perry is crazy. I'm afraid they're going to put her away. You know, in a crazy house. But the thing is killing her, Dex, it's *killing* her."

I was vaguely aware of the restaurant door opening and Rebecca coming out of it. She stood beside me but I couldn't look up at her. I couldn't move. I couldn't even process what was going on. Something had Perry and it was killing her. Something so bad that Ada had to call me – of all people – and ask for *my* help.

"I'll do whatever I can," I told her, trying to get the determination in my voice heard over the phone. "You have to promise to keep her safe until I get there."

"What if I can't? They don't listen to me. They've got her like an animal...and she is an animal, she's an animal now!" Ada broke off as her words got clogged by the tears. Ada was one tough teen cookie. Little fifteen. To hear her cry over Perry put the final dagger into my heart.

"Ada, listen to me. I'm going to take care of this, OK? I'm not going to let anything else happen to her, you understand me? I am going to do whatever it takes to make sure she gets out of this. Give me a day, give me a few hours, I will be there and I will fix her. You understand, little fifteen?"

I heard a sniffle and a pause. Finally she said, "OK. But please hurry."

"I'll text you when I'm on my way," I told her.

"Thank you. Thank you, Dex," she said. "I knew you weren't as big of an asshole as everyone said."

Oh, gee thanks.

"Yeah, well, we'll see. Hold tight, OK?"

"OK, bye."

I never made out my bye before the line went dead. I looked up at Rebecca who was watching me in horror. I was shaking all over.

"I have to go to Perry," I told her, voice wavering. "She's in trouble."

Her eyes widened and then she helped me to my feet before people started thinking I was a crazy street punk.

"Anything I can do?" she asked. I saw the fright in her face. She cared a lot about Perry too. It suddenly hit me how disappointed Rebecca must have been since Perry and I parted. No wonder she went all the way to Portland when I had asked her not to. She was hurting from it too, from the mistakes I made.

I couldn't have felt like more of an ass. More of a horrible human being. Not even. A pig, as Rebecca had said. But I couldn't let myself dwell on it anymore either. I had months of that under my belt. I wanted to better myself. This was the best chance for me to prove myself. It wouldn't undo anything but...I couldn't live with myself if I did nothing. Like it or not – and I certainly didn't like it – Perry was still the most important thing in the world to me. Knowing she was out there was painful enough. But knowing she might not ever be out there again...that was something I couldn't live with.

I shook my head and took Rebecca's hand and kissed it. "Thank you for being there for me, through all of this. I've got a few phone calls and bribes to make, then I'm out of here."

"You'll get her back," she said, even though she couldn't have known what trouble Perry was in. "Then when you do, you're going to bring her here and we'll all have pizza together."

I promised her and ran off down the street, into the dusk.

FIFTEEN

BAILOUT

RAGE MAKES YOU STUPID.

It's one of the things I learned today, along with "trust your instincts" and "shitting in public is impossible."

I'm no stranger to anger problems. I try not to let it rule me though fuck if I don't have a lot of shit to be angry about. But I think I have been pretty good about it. I can blow up on occasion but most of the time I just shove the rage somewhere deep inside. Or I don't even process it at all. Like water off a duck's ass. Back. Whatever.

Before I even pulled the car down Perry's street, I knew the clusterfuckery that lay ahead of us. Not even that, I could *hear* it. Don't ask me how, in fact. In fact, be prepared to not ask me a lot of things. Trust me, I don't have answers. But I could hear, in my head I guess, Max's voice telling everyone to calm down. I could sense a gathering of people, authority figures, more than just her family. So when we came to her house and saw the cop cars, I wasn't all that surprised.

I was just unprepared.

I should have had a better plan than to just get out of

the car and walk toward the house, hand in hand with Perry as a show of solidarity. I just wanted her parents, Max, the cops, to see that I hadn't kidnapped her, she had gone willingly. I selfishly wanted to prove myself to them. And jab them in the eyes a little bit. You know, the whole *oooh but look who your daughter chose in the end, muahaha.*

Yeah, I'm that petty. You should know this by now.

But I was totally unprepared for the reality of everything. Knowing Max and our fucked-up relationship, I still didn't think he would so easily turn on me. Or on her. He was supposed to care about her. For fuck's sake, he stuck his... no, I don't even want to think about it. I'll vomit.

And when Perry's father came roaring for me, Mr. Fists O' Fury, I didn't expect him to be so nuts. Did I deserve the punch? Yes. God, yes. For the way I acted with Perry, after, you know...I totally deserved it. I deserved a thousand of them and under any other circumstance I would have gladly stood in line for a firing squad of fat Italian knuckles. But this wasn't just for that. It was for assuming I had stolen their daughter away, abducted her into the night so I could do all sorts of hellish things to her. In an ideal world I could do hellish things to her and she'd love it but in this world I came to save Perry. No one else seemed to give a shit.

So, stupid me, even though one of my worst-case scenarios involved some police action, I figured I'd be able to talk to them like they were rational human beings. You know, funny story but this is all a BIG misunderstanding and then we'd all laugh about it. I did not expect them to come after me like I'd just assassinated the mayor of Portland.

Click. Click. Two cold, metal handcuffs around the wrist.

I'd never been arrested before but I thought maybe

they'd just tell me to come with them or they'd at least place those plastic cuffs on. I mean, I wasn't a menace to society. But the click, click, was preceded by my arms being grabbed and yanked roughly behind me and followed by a cop reading me my rights.

Part of me felt like laughing at the absurdity of it all and I was this close to telling them to shut up, I'd watched *Law & Order* enough times, I knew my rights. But it was not being arrested that kept the humor sucked out of me. It was feeling utterly helpless as Maximus appeared and went straight for Perry, holding her back with his stupid GI Joe arms.

In that moment time did its funny slow-down dance and all three of us were communicating soundlessly. Both Perry and Max were looking at me and I was torn between trying to figure out what the fuck Max really wanted and letting Perry know she was going to be OK.

The problem was, I was in handcuffs and being shoved toward the cop car. I wasn't even sure if I was going to be OK, how was I going to be sure about her? I was already breaking the promise I made to myself earlier, that I would do absolutely everything in my power to protect her. As if I had some bloody powers, as if I was some kind of hero. All it took was stepping out of the crunched-up Highlander for me to get punched in the face and put in police custody.

Max, never taking his hawk eyes off me, leaned into Perry and whispered into her ear "Don't fight it, Perry, do as I say. I won't let them take you anywhere but you have to play nice and play fair. Calm down." I felt my blood boil hot, my face flushing, burning. He was trying to take my role again, AGAIN! The nerve of that ginger bastard telling Perry, *my* Perry, to calm down, while she was struggling against him.

Perry wasn't having any of it though and I could feel her thoughts slamming at me. She was more worried about me than about herself. Her eyes were wet with unshed tears and vibrant with the same sort of anger that was seething through me.

I'll be fine, I thought hard trying to get the message across the yard with just my eyes. Whether she got the message or not, I didn't know, and it didn't matter because it was suddenly no longer about me.

A tall man with a patronizing tilt of the head and a falsely distinguished style, like a little kid wearing grown-up clothes, came out of the house and calmly walked toward Perry and Max. It was Perry's shrink, Doctor Freebody or whoever. I never met the man but I had met enough shrinks to pick them out in a crowd. This was the enemy and he was here for her.

I must have grunted or cried out and I was trying to get to her but the cops kept me under control. For now.

They pushed me toward the car and shoved me in the back seat. I yelped, twisting in my seat, fighting them, only to see Perry being engulfed by the doctor's shadow. My heart felt shadowed too, a giant eclipse that squeezed the life out of me.

I had lost her once before. I couldn't lose her again.

I thrashed in the seat as the car lurched and roared away from the house and down the street. I was screaming, yelling, the cops were threatening me with things I didn't understand. English was a language I no longer understood. The only thing I heard, the only thing I responded to, was rage.

And rage makes you stupid.

I *knew* it was nearly impossible to escape out of a moving police car. I knew that if I attempted to kick out the side window with both my hands behind me, my feet would either do nothing, or if I was shit-out-of-lucky, I would get one foot stuck in the glass. And then what? Somehow squeeze out of the window while the car is moving at 20 miles an hour?

I knew all these things. But rage doesn't. The power of the anger flowing through me, the urge to get back to Perry while I could, had raised me into another level of consciousness. In other words, I was bat-shit crazy.

Therefore, what happened next was a blur.

With a roar that was neither internal nor external I leaned back in the seat and then propelled my legs forward. My boots met the glass and shattered it with an explosion of light and glitter that filled the car like a snowstorm.

The brakes screeched but the car didn't stop. I didn't have much time. I don't know how I broke the glass so easily and I don't know how I shimmied myself out of the car legs first. I don't know how I was airborne for a few seconds before my shoulder hit the grass at the side of the road and I tumbled along like a rag doll. I don't know how I immediately got to my feet, shaking broken glass out of my hair, and started running back the way we came, not even giving a backward glance to the cop car.

I don't know how any of this happened. All I did know was that I had to get to Perry and get her out of there. If Max, the doctor, *anyone* touched a single hair on her head, I was going to rip shit up. If you think I went Hulk just there, you have no idea. At that moment even I had no idea; I just knew it wasn't going to be pretty.

Unfortunately, even though I felt no pain and was running along with glass streaming off of me, maybe just blocks away from Perry, I was also running with my hands behind my back. It made things a bit awkward. And the closing darkness made things a bit hazy. And my fucking boots that helped me escape the car got caught on the lip of a tree root and went flying for the ground.

Dirt, meet face. That was going to leave a mark.

I groaned and winced, the movement making the dirt-burn on my cheek sting. I had no time to wallow in it. I got up to my feet took a step and heard:

"Freeze!"

Just like in the movies. They actually yelled "freeze." Wish they added "punk" at the end of it.

Also wish I had actually froze on my own accord instead of turning around to face them with a sneer. The officer facing me, who looked suspiciously like that douche from those dance movies, had a look of fear and fire in his face. Oh, and he was holding a taser aimed at me.

I sneered at the taser. In rage mode I didn't think anything could stop me. I began to move.

The next thing I knew there was a crackle of electricity in the air. My body went completely stiff, painfully, unbearably rigid like a board as I felt my muscles being hit by a million sledgehammers. My motor skills ceased to function. I had no control over anything. Now I was frozen and yet completely aware of what was going on at the same time. *Please don't let me shit my pants*, I thought.

I was aware I was getting consistently lower to the ground. Aware that my breath was hitched, my body was convulsing in stretched lines. Aware that the dirt was coming up to meet my face. Again.

As soon as I hit the ground like a sack of potatoes, it stopped and I shot off a round of expletives that would even make non-raging/non-tased Dex blush. The pain was over and I was left feeling like I had been run over by a buffalo stampede...if the buffalo were all live wires.

In my state of total exhaustion, the officers were able to handle me and quickly got me to my feet while they called in another cop car. They seemed scared of their captive and when they brought me toward the car, which had been stopped up the road, I could see why. I saw the damage I did when I hit the ground. I saw the glass shattered at the rear window. I wondered how I managed to pull that off and from the looks I saw the officers shooting each other, I could tell they were wondering the same thing.

I made it back to the police station in a paddy wagon. I suppose now I was a threat, if I wasn't already before. They could throw the book at me for trying to resist arrest, for trying to escape. The rage I felt, the need to get back to Perry, was still there ebbing beneath the surface but the rational part of my noggin at least had some control. My balls had been too big for my britches and now they were barely there. I hoped the tasing didn't do any serious damage.

Once at the station I was put through a round of questioning by some surly-looking individuals. I was photographed – and I smiled through it all (why not, I had a nice smile). I would have thought I'd be shown to a doctor since I had been tased, but they never made any mention of the event and I didn't want to press my luck by bringing it up. I was stripped of all my belongings; my cell phone, my money, my notepad.

Then I was given a *very* thorough pat down. I had wondered if my balls were still around and I can tell you, yes they sure are, Officer Zucotti found them. It was sad that ever since Jenn and I broke up, that *that* was the most action I had gotten. Thank god Zucotti was a gentle beast.

With my dignity and male-groping virginity gone, I was then showed to my cell. The guards took me past the holding cells that were filled with a smorgasbord of Portland's vagrants, criminals and drunks (and there were a lot from each category) and put me in a cell that had only one other guy.

He was sitting on the aluminum shitter and emitting a stench that made my eyes water. It was like a stanky-ass car wreck, I wanted, *needed*, to look away and give the man some privacy but it was fucking hard when the cell only consisted of two concrete slabs with thin mattresses on top and the sink. And the shitter. And the man on the shitter.

I would later find out his name was Gus.

Gus and I had a lovely time bonding. He was huge and wide, like a muscular elephant or Vin Diesel's bigger cousin, and covered with tats from head to toe. They literally went up his neck and onto the giant expanse of his bald head. But he was surprisingly well-spoken. He'd been there all day for violating his parole. I didn't ask what his crime was – I didn't know how to react if he said he'd murdered his landlord or something like that ("Oh, that's cool. Right on."). But he was keen to interrogate me. I guess he felt we had no secrets if I'd seen him shit.

"There's this girl," I started and immediately winced at how cliché that sounded. We were sitting across from each other on the cold mattresses. I had no clue what time it was.

"Isn't there always?" Gus replied. Also cliché.

"Yeah. Well, not usually. Not for me. But she's...she's in a fuckload of trouble."

"Trouble and women go hand in hand." Gus squeezed one of his hands with the others. I heard his bones pop. He smiled, showing blinding white veneers.

"That they do."

I wasn't sure how much I could tell Gus without him

thinking I was crazy but I figured if you can't tell the truth to your fucking cellmate, who can you tell the truth to?

"Did you try and kill her?"

The glib way he said it, glib and utterly sincere, made me raise my brows to the roof.

"No," I said carefully. Though, if the exorcism had failed, wouldn't that have been a consequence? I felt sick at the thought. The smell in here didn't help either.

"I didn't try to kill her. I tried to save her. She was sick. I wasn't around...we had a fight, I guess you could call it."

He nodded knowingly. I didn't like that he was relating to me. It made me wonder just the kind of person I was.

I continued, "And after the fight we didn't speak for a while. She just cut me out of her life. Did I deserve it? Yes. Did I think she'd actually never talk to me again? No. Actually I didn't. You know, she and I...we fight all the time. In small ways. I think it's because we like to push each other's buttons. You know how some people really get under your skin...and you like it? I fucking loved it. She pushed me, poked at me. She questioned me, kicked me, annoyed me. She was always there, digging, digging, digging, and I loved every second of it. I fucking hate talking about myself but she cared so much to get to the bottom of me, like I was some sort of mystery. I don't think I've ever had anyone like that in my whole life, someone who wanted to know you, the real you, and wanted you to be a better person, a better man."

"Did you become a better man?"

I looked down at my hands. Just the other morning I was holding Perry's hand as she slept, not really knowing if she'd ever really wake up. If she'd be the same. Now my hands were dirty and scraped pink from the fall from the police car, my wrists were rubbed raw from the cuffs.

Had I become a better man? That was the question, what it all came down to, wasn't it?

I had done a lot in Perry's absence. There was more change than I was comfortable with. I ended things with Jenn, which was still surprisingly hard considering what we knew about each other. I confessed to being with Perry, she confessed to being with Bradley. Say what you want about our relationship, about Jenn, but a lot of habits were made over the course of three years. Saying goodbye to something or someone after that long of a time, even if it brought you pain and misery, is hard. It's like living with a gangrene foot. You know you need to just whack it off and you'll be healthier for it. But damn if you don't feel some sort of emptiness when your decaying foot is gone. You look at the end of your leg expecting to see it there all black and rotting but there's just nothing but air now. And, if I'm being honest here, I do miss the sex. Anyone would. The earlier pat-down aside, who knew when I'd next get laid? It would be a lot of wishful fucking thinking to imagine it would be Perry.

So there was that. No more long-term girlfriend. No more sex life. Then I listened to the tapes, heard what Pippa told Perry, found out about the switched meds. It made me hate her just a little bit, which lessened the pain of having her gone. Then it made me appreciate what Perry did in her diabolical, scheming little way. She did me a favor. And I let that favor continue. I threw out all my meds. Fuck it all to hell, if I was going to see ghosts, I was going to see ghosts. If they could see me, I decided I'd want to see them. And so far, they'd been kind and few and far between. No sign of the one ghost I hoped I'd never see.

With the medication out of my system, my body responded by piling on some weight. It didn't help that I'd also gone from lying-on-the-bathroom-floor-drinking-Jack-out-of-the-bottle to stuffing every single thing in my face. One month of being depressed and desperate as shit and I was going to make up for it with every food possible. So I started going to the gym and directed some of that weight in the right places. I started training for 10K runs with Dean, started feeling stronger. More capable. More of a man.

I even got a new tattoo, one that would remind me of exactly what was important in my life. And what was worth fighting for, every bitter step of the way.

So was I a better man? The minute I heard from Ada I knew that question would be put to the test. Here was my chance to really come through, to prove myself. I did end up saving Perry. I give myself credit for that. I give her credit for actually allowing me to save her too.

But, didn't I also make things worse? If it hadn't been for me, she wouldn't be alive. But here I was in jail with Gus, unable to help her and she was...fuck. I had no fucking idea where she was. The demon was gone but she had new demons to consider. Ones that wouldn't bow to a shaman. For all I knew, Perry could be walking down the same path that her mother pushed on Pippa. She could be alone at this very instance with no one to look out for her, no one to protect her.

She might not even be the Perry I know anymore, medicated to a point of lifelessness and apathy, the passion and fire sucked right out of her.

The thought rattled me. It really fucking shook my organs, stabbed at my heart, squeezed my lungs until my face grew hot and tense and the volcano inside threatened to cut loose.

I had to get out of there.

"Are you OK man?" Gus asked.

I barely heard him. Panic dulled all my senses.

I got up and all I could think was *GET OUT OF HERE.*

Like a raging robot, I put my hands on both sides of sink...

"No man, she's not worth it," I heard Gus like background music.

...and with a terrifying cry of metal and concrete, I pulled the metal fixture out of the ground. Water gushed straight up in to the cell, soaking me in minutes flat.

I smiled.

Someone yelled, "Guard!"

I think it was Gus.

It didn't matter. I wasn't even sure what I was going to do with myself. In my head I saw myself walking over to the sink and ripping it out of the ground and then throwing it at the bars. The bars would break open and I would walk out, free.

Only I knew that was impossible. Throwing the sink would do nothing to the bars but create a lot of noise and ruin their plumbing. But how the fuck was I holding it in my hands? How did I manage to rip it out of the ground?

My muscles were much bigger and I was stronger, I knew that, but...this?

Before I could even contemplate it further, the cell door slid open and a bunch of yelling guards came in. I felt something hard hit the back of my neck and I was down.

The last thing I remember thinking as I lay on the wet, cold, disgusting ground was that I never answered Gus. I never told him if I was a better man or not.

When I came to, I had a killer headache and I was alone. No more Gus, now I was in another cell. The bars opened up onto a hallway with a guard sitting across from me, which meant I still wasn't using the can in public but at least I no longer had a roommate. Not that Gus was bad, but look where his questions had gotten me.

I rubbed the back of neck, wondering what brutal police instrument came down on me and eyed the guard suspiciously. He returned the favor. I got it. I was more than a troublemaker, I was a force to be reckoned with and I had my own permanent guard. Seemed the more upset I was getting over Perry, the more I was dooming myself to life in prison.

"What time is it?" I asked the guard. My voice sound raw and groggy.

The guard didn't say anything, just kept on giving me the evil eye.

I got up – slowly – feeling all out of sorts.

"Not the talkative type, huh?" I asked. It felt like I'd been in a washing machine with bricks. My clothes were completely dry though, and in the dank jail, I doubted that would have happened fast. I staggered over to the bars and leaned against them, eyeing down the guard. He was a big guy. He didn't flinch. He didn't look away. He was made for this sort of thing.

"Aren't I supposed to get one phone call?"

The guard didn't look away. "Normal perps get them. You ain't normal."

Wasn't that the understatement.

"Is it because I damaged your sink?"

"Not my sink," he said with a haughty sniff. "And it was damaged to begin with. No way you could have pulled that shit out of the ground, so get that higher than thou look off your face and sit your skinny ass back down."

He might have been right about that but I wasn't about to sit down.

"I think I want my phone call."

"No phone calls."

"I think I want to know what time it is."

"Fuck off."

I think I might bend these bars in two, I thought, my hands tightening their grip on them.

Glad I didn't say it out loud. Nothing happened. Hulk I wasn't.

So I continued to stare at the guard. I thought about kicking up a fuss about police brutality and being hit on the head, I thought about threatening them over my right. But thinking didn't do me any good. They would just say it was in self-defense, and who would they ask as a witness? Gus? They'd let him out early if they could get him to twist his version of events around.

I wanted to sigh. I wanted to exhale all the anger and frustration boiling inside of me but that would only show weakness. I wasn't weak. I was going to get out somehow, I just didn't know when.

"Declan Foray?" Someone yelled from down the hall.

My head whipped up as did the guard's. He looked less than pleased.

The Step-Up cop was in front of me with a wary smile on his face. He must have been fantasizing about tasing me again.

"You're free to go, your bail has been posted." He stuck keys in the lock and the door opened.

"What?" I asked, shocked, really.

"You sound as surprised as I was," he commented, grabbing me roughly by the arm and leading me down the hall. I heard the guard growl in my wake.

We came into a room where they gave my meager possessions back and I caught a glimpse of a clock. It was at three. And judging by the dim light that streamed in through the windows as I was escorted into the waiting area, it was three in the afternoon, the next day.

Holy fuck, how long had I been out for?

Not only that but, holy fuck, what the fuck is Ginger Elvis doing here?

Across the room, rising up from his seat, like some redhead giant from Planet Flannel, was Max.

It took every bit of control to keep myself from wrapping my hands around his fat neck and squeezing.

So much control that I could barely move. It was like being tased all over again.

"Don't look so happy to be free," he drawled in his stupid accent. He sauntered over to me and laid his hand on my shoulder. "Would you rather they put you back in there? I still have the receipt."

He waved it in the air with his other hand. I was proud of myself for just swatting away his freckled hand and doing nothing else.

"I could kill you," I said, seething the words through grinding teeth.

"I reckon you shouldn't make such threats in a police station," he said in a lowered voice. He turned and ambled out of the room and into the blowing cold wind outside. "Come on, I'll give you a ride to your car. It's at the impound lot. Did you hit a deer or something?"

I was in no mood to talk to him. I was so fucking angry and relieved at the same time and my feet were itching to take me back to Perry.

We got in his truck and I shuddered at the thought of Perry being in this car with him. I knew she had, I could also smell it. He knew too. He had another idiotic grin on his face.

"You could thank me, ya know," he said as he flipped the engine.

"Where's Perry?"

He narrowed his eyes at me. I narrowed mine right back. As the guard learned, you don't play the glare game with Dex Foray.

Finally he said, "She's fine, don't worry about her."

"Don't worry about her," I growled. "You fucking dick-wad. Because of you, she's in danger."

"She's not in danger," he said, bringing the truck out onto the street. "She's at home and she's fine. And it's because of you this whole mess started in the first place so if I were you, I wouldn't throw stones."

Throw stones? I was beyond throwing stones.

I headbutted him instead.

I felt nothing but pleasure as my head connected with his cheek. He dropped the wheel for a few seconds and the truck wiggled down the lane.

"What the fuck?!" he cried out, reaching for his face with one hand and trying to regain control of the wheel with the other. A few other cars honked in the twilight until the truck was under his control.

"Pull over," I said, my teeth grinding.

"Fuck you."

"Pull. Over."

Max took one look at my face, his eyes watering, and gave in. I was absolutely seething. I didn't want to do anything to him at the police station, but now that we were a few blocks away, there was nothing stopping me from going apeshit on him.

He pulled the truck to the side of the road outside a small house. I wondered if the owners would mind if I murdered someone in their front yard. A big red-headed someone. He was so full of shit, he'd make fantastic fertilizer for their garden.

I reached over and turned off the engine. My fists curled at my side.

"Do you want to do this the easy way or the hard way?" I asked.

"What the hell are you talking about, Dex?" He rubbed at his cheek while looking pained.

"I'm giving you a choice in how you want your ass kicked, *Max*," I replied.

He frowned. "Maximus. It's Maximus. Why do insist on calling me Max?"

"Because that's the name I know you by. I don't know this *Maximus* who fucks me over and sleeps with my... my...woman."

I cringed at the way it came out and knew Max was going to throw it back in my face.

I was right. He laughed without it reaching his eyes. "Your woman? *Your* woman? Oh you've got to be kidding me, man."

"You know what I mean."

"No, actually I don't. I reckon you've got you and Perry's relationship completely wrong. Your *woman* wants nothing to do with you."

"That's not true," I protested. My protest sounded weak and I hated that.

"It is so. Brother, you have no clue what you did, do you?"

"Don't call me Brother," I barked at him.

"Don't call me Max," he shot back.

"I know what I did, all right? It doesn't matter."

He raises his brows to the roof the car. The look said, *holy shit you are in denial*. And I was. But I needed to win this argument. I still wanted to kick his ass and he was distracting me with words.

"If you reckon that it doesn't matter to Perry," he started.

"Get out of the car," I interrupted. "I can't kick your ass in here."

He eyed me wearily. "And why do you want to kick my ass again? Is it because I just bailed you out of fucking jail with my own money?"

Actually, that was part of it. I hated the idea of being in debt to Maximus. Er, Max. Douche.

"I want to kick your ass because you're a traitor, that's why."

He snorted. "Seriously?"

"You took advantage of her." The thought of Max putting his hands on her, his tongue on her...I had to stop thinking about it. If I kept on, Max would be missing his balls.

"I did not," he said. "She wanted it."

"She wasn't herself," I sneered. The anger was getting harder to suppress.

"Well how was I supposed to know that?"

I sat back a bit, feeling smug. "Exactly. You don't know her at all. So you wouldn't know that."

He looked out the window. "And how does that make me a traitor anyway?"

"Have you not heard of something called the Bro's Code?"

He laughed again, this time it shook the car. I had to wait impatiently for him to calm down enough to speak.

"You are really something, you know that pal?" he finally said.

"Fuck off, I'm not your pal."

"And thank god for that. Dex, you slept with *my* girlfriend. Or did you forget that along with everything else from New York?"

"She came on to me." It was true, too. No excuses, but I was in a terrible place when it happened. There was a reason I tried to forget everything that happened in New York. Too many memories. Too many ghosts.

"And Perry came on to me."

I narrowed my eyes at him, searching his face for the truth. His jaw was tense and the skin beside his eye was twitching. I didn't know if it was because I hit him there or that he was lying.

"I highly doubt that," I said, even though my voice wavered with uncertainty. "But even without that, you not only turned on me but you turned on her. She told me everything that happened. You hung her out to dry when she needed you most."

His face went cold. "I did what I had to do."

"What the fuck does that mean? No one said you had to side with her parents and make her look like a nutcase. No one said you had to pretend that all this supernatural stuff was bullshit. No one made you do this stuff. You fucked it up yourself."

He grew silent. I didn't like the silence. I wanted him to come back at me with words. I wanted to keep wanting to hit him.

"That's not true at all," he said quietly. "You have no idea."

"No idea about what? You were being a selfish prick."

"Oh, and you weren't? You destroyed her."

"And you turned her in. Fine pair of men we make."

I clenched my fist and sat back in my seat, suddenly angry at myself as well. All Perry needed –deserved – was a man in her life that would love her, support her and make her his world. He had his chance. So had I. Now I was afraid it was too late.

"Anyway, I didn't turn on her. Her parents wouldn't have believed me at any rate."

I shook my head. "That's not the point. You should have sided with her no matter what the cost."

"The cost would have been greater than you realize," he said. His drawl was low and there was a hard edge to his voice. It commanded my attention.

What the fuck did that mean? I want to ask him that but I wasn't sure what kind of answer I'd get. Something about all of this was tugging at me but my brain couldn't really focus on what or why.

"Why did you come here?" I asked.

He twitched then composed himself. "What do you mean?"

"Why did you come to Portland? Why did you contact Jimmy?"

He shrugged. "I wanted a change of scenery."

I watched him closely. He wasn't meeting my eyes.

"You have good timing, you know that?"

"It depends on what you mean by good," he mused.

"Just funny how I'm out of the picture and you immediately swoop in."

"Hey, I had made plans to come here while you were still...in the picture."

That was true. Jimmy had told Perry and I about Max

153

the night of the Xmas party. The best night of my life turned the worst night of my life. Still...

"And in Red Fox..." I wondered aloud.

Max gave me a funny look. "Red Fox? What about it?"

I didn't know, exactly. I wasn't sure where I was going with it, only that something was off, like a missing puzzle piece. I started to think back about Max and what I actually knew about him. Despite being in a band together, sleeping with his girlfriend, spending most of our NYU days working on the same films, frequenting the same bars, I still didn't know that much about Mr. Maximus Jacobs.

But then again, he could say the same about me.

"Who are you?" I asked, looking him square in the face. "Really?"

He blinked. "Maximus. Just Maximus. Not your buddy. Not your pal."

"Yet, you're always around at the most...pressing moments. Trying to help me out in the most backward way possible."

"Can we go now?" He straightened out his long legs and put his hand on the key. "If you reckon bailing you out of jail is backward helping, you're the one who's got things turned around."

"I don't trust you," I told him but buckled up my seat belt.

"I don't like you."

"Why did you bail me out then?"

He sighed as he started the truck. "Because I like *her*."

His eyes were completely sincere. I know what that look meant. He had it bad for her. Well that made two of us. Whoop dee fucking doo.

"You can't have her, you know," I said. I meant it.

"That will be her choice." He shrugged like it was no big deal. No big deal that he had already lost.

"She already made her choice. I thought that was quite apparent."

"Yeah, well we'll see when she's normal. Which she is now, thank the lord."

I bit my lip and looked out at the darkening afternoon. "How far away is the car?"

"Not far. Then you're free to do whatever you like."

I opened my mouth to speak but he cut me off. "Whatever you like providing you don't go to her."

"Don't you fucking tell me what I can't do."

"I'm not," he said testily. "You reckon her parents are going to welcome you with open arms if you go back there? They'll call the cops again."

"They can't arrest me for visiting."

"I wouldn't press your luck."

"You care about me again?"

"I'm not bailing you out twice."

"You won't have to." I wasn't just going to show up. I brought out my phone and started to text Perry. But I didn't know what to say.

"What are you doing?" Max asked, looking over.

"Do fuck off." I decided to text Ada instead. I wasn't sure where Perry was, if she was OK. Just because Maximus said she was didn't mean it was true. I also didn't know if her psycho parents were monitoring her phone or something.

I texted, *The douchecanoe bailed me out. Where's Perry? Can I see her?*

I waited a few moments for an immediate reply and when I didn't get one, I put the phone back in my pocket.

"Don't do anything stupid," Max warned. "Believe it or

not, I really do care about her. We were lucky that she's fine, that the doctors didn't find anything wrong with her."

"That wasn't luck," I told him. "That was *me*. If I hadn't of showed up..."

"If Ada hadn't reached out to you."

Fuck. I hated it when he was right. I didn't want to think about what would have happened if Ada hadn't called me that day.

Max lowered his voice. "You know I wouldn't have let anything happen to her. I wasn't going to let them put her away. I wasn't going to let it go that far."

"Just far enough, right? And for what reason then?"

"I told you."

"No, you really didn't. You're acting like you're serving some higher purpose here."

A weird thought struck me. Was he serving some other purpose? I squinted at him, taking in the ginger. I thought about what we had talked about minutes earlier. His appearances in my life. His "ghost-hearing" abilities. Some things fit together, some things didn't.

He didn't say anything. I was tempted to ask the "who are you" question again but I knew it would get me nowhere. He was my old college buddy Max, that's all he could be. That's all I wanted him to be.

My phone beeped and I jumped in my seat. Everything had me on edge.

I looked at the text from Ada: *WTF?! OK I'm glad ur out. She's OK - sleeping. Maybe come by around 11 when the rents R asleep.*

The thought of Perry lying in her bed, sleeping, brought a smile to her face. As creepy as it sounds, there had been so many times I'd watched her sleep. Just a ratty Slayer concert tee, bedhead, no makeup. She looked so beautiful, so serene, even when she was drooling.

My heart flipped in my chest, a mix of hope and sadness. I swallowed the feeling and buried it by telling myself I was going to do whatever it took to make things right between us again.

Whatever it took.

AFTERWORD

In case you haven't noticed, almost all of the chapter titles are songs. Favorites of mine, actually. Check them out:

- After School Special – Mr. Bungle (too weird? Listen to Retrovertigo instead)

- Spookshow Baby – Rob Zombie

- Even Deeper – Nine Inch Nails

- Big Dumb Sex – Soundgarden

- Butterfly Caught – Massive Attack

- She's Got a Way – Billy Joel

- Stripsearch - Faith No More (the song playing during the scene)

- Digging the Grave – Faith No More

- When Good Dogs Do Bad Things – Dillinger Escape Plan

- She Loves Me Not – Faith No More

- Maxwell's Silver Hammer – The Beatles

- Mr. Self-Destruct – Nine Inch Nails

- Demon Cleaner/Bailout - – Kyuss

Actually, just play Nine Inch Nails, all albums, on shuffle...THAT is Dex's mind.

ALSO BY KARINA HALLE

A Nordic King

Nothing Personal

My Life in Shambles

Discretion

Disarm

Disavow

The Royal Rogue

The Forbidden Man

Lovewrecked

One Hot Italian Summer

The One That Got Away

Romantic Suspense Novels by Karina Halle

Sins and Needles (The Artists Trilogy #1)

On Every Street (An Artists Trilogy Novella #0.5)

Shooting Scars (The Artists Trilogy #2)

Bold Tricks (The Artists Trilogy #3)

Dirty Angels (Dirty Angels #1)

Dirty Deeds (Dirty Angels #2)

Dirty Promises (Dirty Angels #3)

Black Hearts (Sins Duet #1)

Dirty Souls (Sins Duet #2)

Horror Romance

Darkhouse (EIT #1)

Red Fox (EIT #2)

The Benson (EIT #2.5)

ABOUT THE AUTHOR

Karina Halle, a former screenwriter, travel writer and music journalist, is the *New York Times*, *Wall Street Journal*, and *USA Today* bestselling author of *The Pact*, *A Nordic King*, and *Sins & Needles*, as well as over fifty other wild and romantic reads. She, her husband, and their adopted pit bull live in a rain forest on an island off British Columbia, where they operate a B&B that's perfect for writers' retreats. In the winter, you can often find them in California or on their beloved island of Kauai, soaking up as much sun (and getting as much inspiration) as possible. For more information, visit

www.authorkarinahalle.com